Owain Glyn Dŵr

The Last Prince of Wales

Owain Glyn Dŵr

The Last Prince of Wales

Peter Gordon Williams

Dedicated to the memory of my parents
Doris and Leyshon Williams

First impression: 2011

Cover illustration: William Rathbone

ISBN: 9 781 84771 363 6

FSC

Published and printed in Wales
on paper from well maintained forests by
Y Lolfa Cyf., Talybont, Ceredigion SY24 5HE
e-mail ylolfa@ylolfa.com
website www.ylolfa.com
tel 01970 832 304
fax 832 782

Owain Glyn Dŵr

His grave is beside no church neither under the shadow of any ancient yew. It is in a spot safer and more sacred still. Rain does not fall on it, hail nor sleet chill nor sere soil above it. It is forever green with the green of eternal spring. Sunny the light on it; close and warm and dear it lies, sheltered from all storms, from all cold or grey oblivion. Time shall not touch it; decay shall not dishonour; for that grave is in the heart of every true Cymro. There for ever, from generation unto generation, grey Owain's heart lies dreaming on, safe for ever and for ever.

Owen Rhoscomyl

Characters

FAMILY

Owain Glyn Dŵr	The Last True Prince of Wales
Margaret Hanmer	The Arglwyddes, Owain's wife
Gruffydd	His eldest son
Maredudd	His youngest son
Catherine	His youngest daughter
Alys	Another daughter
Tudor ap Griffith	Owain's brother
John Hanmer	Owain's brother in law
Edmund Mortimer	Married to Catherine
Sir John Scudamore	Married to Alys
John Scudamore	Owain's young grandchild
William ap Tudor	Cousin of Owain
Rhys ap Tudor	Brother of William

SUPPORTERS

Rhisiart ab Owen	Owain's secretary
Rhys Gethin	Owain's Chief Captain
Griffith Young	Owain's Chancellor
Walter Brut	A Lollard
Alice	Walter's wife
Crach Ffinnant	Owain's Prophet
Iolo Goch	Owain's Bard
Madoc ap Gruffydd	Owain's bodyguard
Henry Don of Kidwelly	Cavalry Captain
John ap Thomas	Conscripted soldier

Hywel ap Madoc	Dean of St Asaph
Archdeacon of Bangor	
Sir John Oldcastle	In the service of King Henry IV
Father Huw	A Franciscan Monk
Henry Percy	Known as Hotspur
Lord Northumberland	Hotspur's father
Travers	Servant to Northumberland
Lord Bardolf	Former counsellor

KING RICHARD'S SUPPORTERS

King Richard II
Duke of Aumerle
Bishop of Carlisle
Earl of Salisbury
Duke of York

OWAIN'S FOES

Henry Bolingbroke	Becomes Henry IV
Prince Hal	Becomes Henry V
David Gam	Lord of Brecon
Hywel Sele	Baron of Nannau
Reginald Grey	Lord of Ruthin
John Massy	Constable of Conway Castle
Hopkin ap Thomas	Prophet of Gower
Constable of Welshpool Castle	
John Rokeby	High Sheriff of Yorkshire
Hugh Burnell	Shrewsbury
John Talbot	Son of Richard Talbot
Adam of Usk	Ecclesiastical Lawyer

THE FRENCH COURT

Charles VI	King of France
Pierre Salmon	Secretary to Charles
Oliver de Clisson	Friend of Charles
Duke of Burgundy	Claimant to the title of Regent
Louís Duke of Orleans	Brother of Charles

FRENCH MILITARY

Count of La Marche
Jean de Hangest
Jean de Roux
Renault de Tire
Patrouillart de Tire
Robert de la Heuzé

CHAPTER 1

Régime change

I T WAS A sultry day in July, 1399, when King Richard, returning from a disastrous campaign in Ireland, disembarked on the coast of west Wales. He was accompanied by the Bishop of Carlisle and the Duke of Aumerle. They were escorted by a small band of dishevelled soldiers whose flags swayed listlessly in the indolent breeze. Richard knelt on one knee and gathered up a handful of sand.

'Oh! The joy of leaving those fetid Irish bogs and standing once more upon my kingdom,' he murmured softly. Then, drawing himself up to his full height and gazing imperiously towards the horizon, he continued, 'Though rebels wound me with their calumnies, the God that made me King has the power to keep me King. For all the men that perfidious Bolingbroke has pressed to raise their steel swords against our golden crown, God has for Richard provided a host of sturdy Welshmen, under the command of the valiant Glendower.'

Aumerle stepped forward and, with the elaborate courtesy practised in Richard's dissolute but punctilious court, bowed low and asked, 'Your Majesty, is this not the very place where faithful Glendower vowed to attend upon your Majesty?'

'Yes indeed, Aumerle.'

'Then, Majesty, he appears to be conspicuous by his absence.'

'Have faith. Glendower served me loyally in the Scottish campaigns. Often I saw him driving those murderous Scottish barbarians before him armed only with a shattered lance. He will come. Look, even as I speak, a horseman spurs towards us.'

It was only when the rider was almost upon them that they realised it was the Earl of Salisbury. The horse reared up on its hind legs as Salisbury tugged on the reins and brought the steed to a juddering halt. Hastily dismounting, Salisbury approached the King, who stepped forward and said, 'Welcome, my good Lord. How far off lies Glendower and his force?'

'Alas, Sire! I can speak only of despair. Had you come but a day earlier you would have had two thousand Welsh bowmen awaiting your command. But yesterday, hearing that you had been slain, the Welshmen have dispersed, some are gone to offer their services to Bolingbroke the rest have followed Glendower to his mountain fastness.'

'Bolingbroke, Bolingbroke! How I hate that accursed name.'

'Since landing, Bolingbroke has gained the support of the Earl of Northumberland and of your uncle the Duke of York. He is now marching in triumph across England towards Wales. He says that his sole aim is to reclaim the title Duke of Lancaster and the estates due to him now that his father, John of Gaunt, is dead. But many believe that it is his ambition to usurp your throne.'

'How I regret the banishment I imposed on him and the seizure of his rightful inheritance. For now it would seem I am about to lose my crown.'

The bishop stepped forward and, after kissing Richard's hand, said, 'Courage, Your Majesty, not all the water of the rough rude sea can wash the balm from an anointed king.'

'My Lord Bishop, you do well to chide me. I am elected King by God and all honour and privilege flow from me. Bring the horses, we will ride to Flint Castle, there to confront this usurper Bolingbroke.'

Owain Glyn Dŵr, known by the English as Glendower, was riding home, not to his elegant moated mansion at Sycharth but to his fortress at Glyndyfrdwy. Behind him marched the men who had remained loyal to their lord, while at his side rode Rhys Gethin, his chief captain.

Above average height, Owain sat upright in the saddle. He wore high, tightly-fitting chamois leather shoes; over his breastplate, upon which was emblazoned a single black lion rampant, he wore a flowing moss-green mantle richly embroidered in silver, clasped by a massive gold brooch. His grey beard was forked and carefully trimmed. A twisted rope of gold adorned his brow and from his belt hung a short two-edged sword. His forehead was low and broad, the hair thick and wavy. His eyes were the colour of the iridescent sea, sometimes green and sometimes grey. He gave the overall impression of a man who was both regal and chivalrous.

Having skirted the Forest of Chirk and forded the river Dee, the party came in sight of the great circular stockade of Glyndyfrdwy. This stockade, consisting of enormous planks of wood built upon a massive stone foundation, enclosed Owain's residence together with a large collection of outbuildings, guest-houses and stables. Owain's dwelling was two stories high, the upper one for the women of the family and their female attendants while a considerable proportion of the lower consisted of an enormous hall, strewn with bracken. In the centre burned an open fire around which at night, when the tables had been cleared, the whole company of warriors and their retainers could sleep.

That evening in the great hall, Owain sat at high table with his family while his warriors drank and caroused before him. Seated at his right-hand was his wife Margaret, the daughter of the distinguished lawyer and confidant of King

Richard, Sir David Hanmer. The Arglwyddes, as she was known, was a stout lady of noble bearing. Her daughter Catherine, pale and slender sat demurely beside her. Two of Owain's sons, Gruffydd and Maredudd, the eldest and youngest respectively, sat on his left. The contrast between the brothers could not have been more marked – Gruffydd dressed in a sober costume cut from rough dark cloth, Maredudd in a short crimson tunic and tight-fitting yellow hose. Gruffydd stared round the hall with hostility while Maredudd's young face evinced a sheepish discomposure at the extravagance of his costume. Owain's other sons were dispersed anonymously among the throng.

The Arglwyddes came from a family who, though English in origin, had long been settled in Wales and had intermarried with their Welsh neighbours. David Hanmer, who had died three years previously, had forged a strong bond between Owain Glyn Dŵr and the Hanmer family. His sons, Gruffydd, John and Philip, maintained that bond after his death and were numbered among Owain's most fervent supporters.

During the boisterous proceedings, Owain glanced uneasily at his other daughter Alys who sat a considerable distance from the Arglwyddes, her face the very personification of bored disdain. Unlike Catherine, who revelled in the bustling life of a functioning fortress, Alys found such an existence rough and repellent.

Owain felt some sympathy for the girl, when he remembered his gilded youth at the court of King Richard. How Alys would have flourished in its elegance and sophistication.

When he expressed these thoughts to the Arglwyddes, she said sharply, 'She is a warrior's daughter and must come to terms with her situation.'

Owain replied, 'But will she? I fear that one day we will lose her.'

Despite the dishes of steaming meat stew and the freely flowing wine, the news that King Richard had been slain on a battlefield in Ireland hung like a shroud upon the company. Owain called for his old friend and poet, Iolo Goch, to entertain the company. The bard, now well advanced in years and looking as fragile as a small bag of bird bones, took up his harp and proceeded to sing stories of romance from the *White Book of Rhydderch*. The warriors listened with rapt attention to his songs of romance and nationhood. When he reached the end of his recital, Iolo paused and, rising from his chair, sang out in a voice that belied his great age the words:

Many a time have I desired
To see a king of our kin.

The hall erupted in a tempest of cheering and stamping feet. Gruffydd and Maredudd looked intently at their father but Owain's face was impassive as he raised his hand and summoned Crach Ffinnant, the bard of Derfel. Iolo was gently shepherded to the side of the hall and Crach took his place. Crach's face was disfigured by a number of hideous birthmarks and he had one serviceable eye that glowed a luminous blue. His grotesque appearance earned him the nickname the Scab.

He sang of Prince Derfel the Mighty, who as a young man joined the court of the ageing High-King Arthur and fought for him at the fateful battle of Camlann. He was one of the few survivors and the bloodshed he had seen made him turn to religion. He forsook the life of a fearsome warrior to become a hermit and monk at Llanderfel in the county of Gwynedd. On his death a massive wooden statue of him riding a horse was erected in Llanderfel church and became possessed of magical powers.

During the recital a soldier entered the hall, largely unobserved, and spoke urgently to Gruffydd who in turn went to his father and whispered in his ear.

Owain said quietly, 'Bring Maredudd, Rhys and this fellow to my chamber. We must discuss how to handle this.' He then hurriedly left the hall.

Owain's chamber was illuminated by the light from five fiercely burning torches. As Gruffydd, Maredudd, Rhys and the messenger entered the room, Owain rose from behind a massive oak desk to greet them. He had changed into a long black silk gown ornamented with strange characters. There were two objects in the room which seemed out of place in the study of a Welsh baron. Under the window an enormous crystal ball rested on an ebony pedestal and on the wall behind the desk hung a large white board on which were inscribed a series of astrological symbols. The remaining walls were lined with shelves on which jostled dusty manuscripts and heavy leather-bound books.

Owain addressed the messenger, 'You have the advantage, as I do not know your name, while you obviously know mine.'

'Madoc ap Gruffydd, Sire. I've the honour of being a member of your honourable company of bowmen.'

'Well Madoc, give me your news.'

'When you left Conway on hearing the news that King Richard had been slain, our captain Rhys Gethin ordered me to stay in the vicinity and report back if anything developed. Well, the very next day Richard with a small escort landed on the beach!'

'Are you sure it was Richard?'

'Yes, Sire. I recognised that tall elegant figure and the mass of yellow hair. King Richard is alive.'

Rhys Gethin pushed forward and asked eagerly, 'You spoke with him?'

'Yes indeed,' Madoc answered proudly, 'and with the Bishop, and Duke Aumerle and the Earl of Salisbury. Never before have such exalted persons spoken to the likes of me.'

'Yes,' Owain said patiently. 'But what news did you glean?'

'That, though King Richard has survived, his army is destroyed in Ireland. That Bolingbroke is marching across Wales towards Flint castle, gathering strength on his way. King Richard is resolved to confront the usurper at Flint and he calls on his friend Glendower to come to his aid. That is the message I bring you, Lord Owain Glyn Dŵr.'

Rhys, unable to contain his excitement, cried out, 'I'll muster the men my lord and we'll start our march to Flint within the hour.'

This was followed by a chorus of approval from the others in the room, apart from Owain who stood silent and impassive. Seeing Owain's reaction, they too fell silent and gazed expectantly at their leader.

Owain spoke with great deliberation. 'Long before we reach Flint the battle will have been lost and won. It pains me to say it, but in the heavens Bolingbroke's star is ascending while Richard's is falling. Bolingbroke is fated to become King Henry IV; why risk the enmity of a new king by a forlorn attempt to rescue one that is doomed? We will not march on Flint. Leave me now.'

Puzzled and subdued, the others left the room. Owain stood transfixed in the centre of his study as if the mind had left the body and was revisiting images of the past. He had spent his youth and early manhood in London. After seven years at the Inns of Court, which had proved more of a social education than a vocational one, he turned from law to the profession of arms. This gave him entry to Richard's court where he became an intimate of the King. Despite Richard's narcissistic tendencies, Owain admired the King's lofty concept of the royal office. When Richard went off on his Scottish wars, Owain accompanied him and fought at his side. At the battle of Berwick, wearing the scarlet feather of a flamingo in his helmet, he fought with the tenacity of a tiger and though unhorsed drove the enemy from the field.

Owain suddenly came to life and moved to the giant globe on its ebony stand. Peering into its depth he gave a wry smile and said, 'As opaque as ever. We will try the mettle of this Henry IV and if we find him wanting, then will we raise the flag of rebellion.'

★

When Richard and his dejected followers reached the high walls of Flint castle, the seneschal threw open the gates and welcomed them in. On hearing that Bolingbroke was advancing on the castle with an army that grew with every stride it made, Richard addressed his bedraggled band of pikemen, 'I discharge you. Hence away.'

One of the men stepped forward and in a voice hoarse with emotion, said, 'We'll defend you to the death, Sire.'

Richard smiled sadly and said, 'Good lads, but I will offer no resistance. Hence away! Flee Richard's dark night and live to see Bolingbroke's bright day.'

Richard, Bishop Carlisle, Aumerle and Salisbury retired to the castle keep. There to await proud Bolingbroke. They did not have to wait long. With drums beating and banners flying, Bolingbroke's army marched through the open gates of the castle and came to a halt in the base court. Bolingbroke did not possess a commanding physical presence. His one distinguishing feature was the contrast between the neat, pointed beard that covered his chin and the luxuriant moustache that flourished beneath his aquiline nose.

Bolingbroke turned to York and Northumberland and said, 'So the Welshmen are dispersed and Richard now hides his head in this undefended castle.'

The Duke of York shook his head sadly and murmured, 'It would have been more seemly, my lord, if you had said King Richard.'

'You mistake my intention. It was only to be brief that I left his title out.'

Standing next to Northumberland was his eldest son Henry Percy, a young man of unwieldy bulk with gleaming dark eyes. Bursting with agitation he blurted out, 'Why keep up this p-pretence of Richard's kingship. Yonder castle houses no king, the King stands here beside us in the base court. Otherwise why have we embarked on this hazardous enterprise?'

Bolingbroke barked out, 'Silence Hotspur, I come to claim only what is my right.'

'The dukedom of Lancaster, I p-presume,' Percy stammered.

York nodded his head vigorously and said, 'That and no more, else you would not have gained my support.'

Bolingbroke turned away and did not respond.

It was at that moment that Richard and his retinue appeared on the ramparts. It could be said that nothing so became his kingship as the leaving of it. He had shaken off his previous melancholy and now stood tall staring down haughtily at Bolingbroke and his followers. Several minutes passed before Richard cried out, 'Bolingbroke, we are amazed at how long we have stood waiting for the fearful bending of your knee. We thought ourselves to be your lawful King.'

Bolingbroke made a contemptuous, barely perceptible genuflection and said, 'Your most obedient subject requests that you descend to the base court so that he may humbly kiss your royal hand. Be assured that my coming hither has no further scope than to claim my rightful inheritance.'

Hotspur whispered in his father's ear, 'By which he means the crown of England.'

Richard and his retinue descended to the base court where he was greeted by Bolingbroke with the words, 'Sire, we come but to escort you to London.'

Richard replied bitterly, 'We must do what force will make us do. Set on towards London, cousin, is it so?'

'Yes, my good lord.'

'Then I must not say no.'

So on that fateful day, Richard set out on a journey that led to his deposition and death. On October 13th, 1399, Henry Bolingbroke was crowned at Westminster Abbey. The following February, to protect his crown, Henry had Richard murdered at Pontefract Castle. The age of Henry IV had dawned.

CHAPTER 2

Brut seeks sanctuary

MASTER RHISIART KNOCKED robustly on the door of Owain's chamber. The young Oxford scholar had learnt during his year's service as Glyn Dŵr's secretary that it was not wise to barge into his master's sanctum without first seeking permission. Standing expectantly behind Rhisiart was a man who was rather older and most emphatically taller. Neither of these attributes constituted the significant difference between these two men. Rhisiart could not be said to possess a handsome countenance, though his dark flashing eyes gave his hooked-nosed face a brutal vitality. His companion's demeanour radiated a saintly benevolence and he possessed the face of an angel.

An irritable, 'Enter', came from behind the door, and, when they obeyed, they were confronted with a man who had obviously been disturbed in his studies and resented the fact.

'Well what is it? More bad news about that land robber Grey?'

'No, my lord,' Rhisiart answered hurriedly, 'I have here Master Walter Brut, a layman of the diocese of Hereford. He comes here seeking your protection.'

Owain eyed Brut suspiciously and barked, 'Protection from what?'

'Religious persecution, my lord,' Brut answered gently. 'You see I'm a Lollard and, some years ago, was tried for heresy before the Bishop.'

Rhisiart broke in eagerly, 'Walter conducted his own

defence, and was acquitted. The proceedings are recorded in the episcopal records.'

'Then why does he now seek protection?' Owain asked.

Walter sighed and answered, 'Because, now that Henry is on the throne, religious intolerance has intensified and I'm once more in danger.'

Owain gestured with his hand and said, 'Sit, we'll discuss this further.'

Walter, rather self-consciously, settled into a chair alongside Rhisiart while Owain sat behind his desk and gazed at Walter with newly awakened interest.

'So you are a Lollard, Master Brut,' he challenged. 'I hope you don't think that I'm one. I tell you what I am, a simple soldier and no theologian. I'm an orthodox Catholic and in this unfortunate schism I owe allegiance to Pope Boniface in Rome and not to that antichrist Benedict in Avignon. Tell me Master Brut, what are the basic tenets of your sect?'

Walter answered without hesitation, 'We deny the doctrine of transubstantiation and stress the importance of preaching and the primacy of scripture as the source of Christian doctrine.'

'Can you give me some instances where these beliefs contradict the teaching of the church?'

'Lollards believe that Christian baptism is of no value if done by a priest living in sin.'

'But that's ridiculous,' exploded Owain. 'What father, anxious to save the soul of a dying infant, would bother himself about the sin of an officiating priest, who is the mere conduit of the divine mercy.'

Undeterred, Walter continued, 'We believe that after the words of consecration the bread remains bread and nothing more.'

'That is a denial of the Miracle of the Mass, the supreme article of our faith.'

Walter continued, 'We believe that the decisions of popes have no value unless they are grounded expressly on Holy Scripture.'

Owain raised his hands and said, 'The Catholic faith subsumes the inevitable contradictions and paradoxes of the human mind. It is at once at the centre and the circumference wherein the pendulum of our poor reason oscillates.'

'I believe that only in the Holy Scriptures, reasonably interpreted, will be found the truth.'

Owain stood up and with a smile said, 'We'll never agree on religious matters, Master Brut, but I welcome you to my dwelling and whatever protection it may afford you. No man should be persecuted for his beliefs, no matter how bizarre they may be.'

Rhisiart interjected, 'Master Brut has his wife Alice with him.'

Owain responded, 'I welcome her too. Ask the Arglwyddes to find Alice a space in the woman's quarters. I know your leader, John Oldcastle. We were students of law at the Middle Temple and, though he was my junior by a number of years we became firm friends. It is a rapport that has survived even though he now holds a notable position in King Henry's service and is a close companion of Prince Hal.'

'John Oldcastle believes in the sacraments and the necessity of penance and confession, but, as a true Lollard, he believes that to put faith or trust in images is the great sin of idolatry.'

Owain smiled indulgently and said, 'We had many animated discussions on those very points. As a young man, no one was more slim and elegant than John but I fear years of indulgence have greatly enlarged his person and some have had the temerity to suggest that he now resembles a tub of lard. Be that as it may, his intelligence burns as brightly as ever. Now you must leave me.'

Throughout this conversation, unnoticed by Brut, a soldier, as sturdy as a young oak, stood impassively in a dark corner of the room. A large axe rested against his right leg. He was Madoc ap Griffith, the soldier who, over a year ago, had brought the news of King Richard's arrival at Flint, news that had forced Owain to make a vital choice. He had decided to abandon Richard to his fate, a decision that, in view of King Henry's increasing intransigence, Owain was beginning to regret. Owain had taken an instant liking to the youth and had made him his personal bodyguard.

When Rhisiart and Brut had left, Owain called to Madoc, 'Come and sit here.'

Although they had often talked together, this was the first time that Owain had invited Madoc to sit with him. Madoc, carrying his axe, moved to a chair and sat with the axe across his knees.

Owain exclaimed, 'Why must you always have that axe within reach?'

Madoc mumbled, 'For your protection, my lord.'

'Yes but surely here in the heart of my family fortress.'

'Could often be the most dangerous place.'

Owain said with a chuckle, 'You could be right. But why is the axe your weapon of choice?'

'I know that I will never leave a foe lying wounded. He will always be dead.'

'That's very humane of you Madoc. I don't suppose a plain warrior such as yourself gives much thought to what in the past created the circumstances we now find ourselves in?'

'Seize the day and to hell with what came before. That's my motto.'

'Take the dispute between Lord Grey and myself. Many years ago when the Anglo Saxons ruled England, Wales was an independent country divided into a number of little kingdoms ruled by petty princes, but when the Normans invaded and William the Conqueror took the English crown, he placed powerful Norman lords along the Welsh border. Over time these lords thrust forward from their border bases into Wales, where they built the castles we see today. Around these castles they created little enclaves and imported citizens for these little towns. This area of Norman lordships became known as the Marches. The Marcher lords, while nominally owing allegiance to the King of England were to all intents and purposes independent and were often at war with each other. Grey holds the lordship of Dyffryn Clwyd while I am Lord of Cynllaith Owain and Glyn Dyrdwy.'

'You are no Norman,' Madoc protested. 'I've heard it said that both on your father's and mother's side you are descended from the Welsh princes.'

Owain laughed and said, 'Not all Welsh barons lost their lands when Wales lost its independence. To return to the dispute I have with Grey. He has seized some land that I claim is mine. We both have appealed to Henry, as he is our Sovereign, and await his verdict. I fear Henry will support Grey, who in addition to his holdings in Wales has wide possessions in the East of England.'

'How I wish our country free from the English yoke, with you as our rightful prince.'

'Back in the twelfth century at a time when Henry II

was leading a military expedition into Wales, he was told by a prisoner, "This ancient land will never be destroyed by the wrath of man. On the Day of Judgment, no other race than the Welsh, or any other language, will give answer to the Supreme Judge for this small corner of the earth.'"

'I say Amen to that,' roared Madoc.

★

Richard's death and Bolingbroke's usurpation had caused great perturbation throughout the land, particularly in Wales. The new King met resistance from the barons, and the Franciscans were so affronted that their monks spread dissent among the common people. Those near Owain urged him to take advantage of the temper of the times and raise the banner of revolt. Among these advisors, in addition to his sons, Gruffydd and Maredudd, were his brother Tudor ap Griffith, his secretary Rhisiart, Master Brut, Captain Rhys Gethin and a fanatical Franciscan monk Father Huw. They impressed on Owain that there would never be a better time to raise his standard of a red dragon on a white background and free Wales from the English yoke.

Owain was motivated by the knowledge that in the twelfth century there had been a completely independent sphere of Welsh influence. It consisted of three kingdoms, Gwynedd, Powys and Deheubarth, ruled respectively from three principal seats – Aberffraw, Mathrafal and Dinefwr. He considered that it was his destiny to restore that golden age and unite the three kingdoms under his rule.

Owain spent fever-racked hours alone in his chamber, scanning the mystical papers spread on his desk and gazing frantically into the depths of his great crystal sphere, while the faithful Madoc stood guard at the door.

'To what end? To what end?' Owain murmured in despair. 'The ancient manuscripts just confuse me. And all I can see in the globe is a swirling atrocity of blood and ashes.'

A great anger against his fate swept over Owain. He strode to the door and called Madoc into the room. Pointing to the great globe he ordered Madoc to smash it to pieces with his axe. It took three mighty blows before the glass shivered into pieces. Owain helped Madoc gather up the splinters into a black velvet drape. After Madoc had left with the debris, Owain regained his composure. He had come to a decision. He would send out orders that all fencible men in Gwynedd and Powys were to attend a levee at his fortress Glyndyfrdwy on the morning of September 16th, in the year 1400.

CHAPTER 3
Owain ignites rebellion

T HAT DAY DAWNED gloriously to reveal a be-flagged tent of enormous size set in the meadow alongside the river. Within this pavilion, Owain stood on a raised platform and gazed down on the seething cauldron of upturned faces that swirled about the dais. He nervously fingered his brow as he felt the weight of the old coronet of solid gold that Hywel ap Madoc, Dean of St Asaph, had dug out from the clutter in the cathedral crypt. His waist was girded by the sword of Elisedd ap Gwylog, the eigthth-century leader who drove, with fire and sword, the English from the land of Powys.

A great roar swept up from the crowd, 'Long live Owain, Prince of Powys.'

Then like storm waves crashing in rapid succession upon a rock, 'Long live Owain, Prince of Gwynedd. Long live Owain, Prince of Powys. Long live Owain, Prince of Deheubarth.'

There was a pause then came, in a crescendo of emotion, 'Long live Owain, Prince of Wales.'

Owain glanced across to where his wife was standing among her ladies. She was smiling and proudly holding the new banner that she had embroidered for the occasion. It was then he noticed that the dragon, instead of being red, was gold.

'Still, gold is her favourite colour,' he thought indulgently.

Owain unsheathed his sword and flourished it above his head, causing the crowd to fall silent.

'I have a vision,' he declared. 'A vision of a Welsh race liberated from the bondage of our English enemies. After many years of captivity, the hour of freedom has now struck. Let not cowardice and sloth deprive our nation of a victory which is in sight. I tell you that when the Welsh students in Oxford and Cambridge and the Welsh labourers in England hear of our rebellion, they will leave their studies, leave their labours and flock to join us. I believe that I am the deliverer appointed by God to lead you to the Promised Land.'

This was greeted with renewed cheering and Owain lowered his sword arm before raising it again so that his sword pointed straight at the rising sun.

Firmly he made a solemn vow, 'I, Owain Glyn Dŵr, swear before all here that I will not sheath my sword or cease from battle till there is not a castle in Wales under any other flag but the dragon.'

Some present noted that though the crowd had proclaimed him Prince of Wales, Owain in his speech made no such claim. The wily statesman was determined to leave himself room for manoeuvre in any future negotiations with Henry.

That night, as the riotous celebrations continued, Owain, eschewing an escort, rode out onto the bare uplands of the Berwyn Range. Once over the mountain, he took the path through the forest that led to the ruins of the ancient city of Mathrafal. When he reached the mound of great stones that marked the entrance to the city, he dismounted and stood in the moonlight with head bowed. With that inward eye he saw the granite walls and marble towers rise once again on the fern strewn forest floor. He saw the four great highways leading to this place from the four quarters of the horizon.

Raising his head, Owain spoke as if in a trance. 'This primeval city had housed a people who had been there since the beginning of time – long before the coming of Christ and Caesar. A people whose souls conquered our fathers' souls as our fathers' swords cut them down.'

A shiver passed through his body as he realised that here on this spot the soul of the ancient Welsh race lay buried. The time had come to bring it back to life.

'Am I the man to do it?' Owain cried.

★

Early one morning a group of six horsemen, under a flag of truce, appeared before the gates of Glyndyfrdwy. At their head was a knight of such prodigious size that the poor horse on which he sat sagged beneath the colossal weight, its legs buckling.

The guards were startled when the knight bellowed out with a voice of thunder, 'Tell Glendower that his erstwhile drinking companion and opponent in many invigorating debates has come to parley.'

On meeting, the two old friends greeted each other joyfully and embraced warmly.

'John, John,' Owain said happily. 'How good to see your dear countenance again, though you have increased in girth since we last met.'

'All the more for you to love, my dear friend,' Oldcastle replied. 'I often think back to those days at the Inns of Court – the cheap beer and the willing lasses.'

A look of concern passed over Owain's face and he said hurriedly, 'The days that are no more.'

Oldcastle echoed him, 'The days that are no more.'

'We are men of destiny now and grapple with grave matters.'

Oldcastle now realised that Owain did not want any of his

earlier indiscretions to tarnish his image as a future Prince of Wales.

He therefore stopped his reminiscing and immediately got down to the reason for his visit. 'Owain, I come as an emissary from King Henry with an ultimatum – you must abandon your claim to the governance of Wales and abort this rebellion. Obey Henry and he will pardon you and your followers, and intervene on your behalf in the dispute with Lord Grey.'

'And if I do not comply with this demand,' Owain asked calmly.

'Henry will muster an army, the like of which you have never dreamed in your worst nightmare, and will hammer you into submission.'

'I have set my hand to the plough and there is no going back now.'

'Please Owain heed my advice, take the pardon or you will be destroyed.'

'There comes a time when one must hazard all for a cause that one believes in. In the future, you might have to make a choice between your King and your faith as a Lollard.'

Owain paused and, before continuing, grasped Oldcastle's hand. 'Now I have a personal favour to ask of you. It concerns my daughter Alys. Unlike Catherine, she is of a reserved and delicate nature and is most unsuited to the rough environment of a castle, especially when it is under siege, as this castle will soon be if Henry is true to his word. I ask you to take her to your family home in Almeley where she will be secure and far happier.'

'My dear friend, take it as done. I will shelter Catherine also.'

'No, Catherine wishes to stay at her father's side.'

At the banquet that night, Owain was amused to see the

animated conversation between Oldcastle and Walter Brut, the latter's eyes shining with excitement as he spoke to the leader of his movement. The Arglwyddes and Catherine sat silent, saddened by the knowledge that Alys would be leaving. Alys remained as inscrutable as ever.

In the morning, as Owain helped Alys mount her horse, he whispered, 'I understand.'

Alys turned her head and looked him fully in the face. He saw that her eyes glistened with tears.

★

The next day Owain held a council of war in his 'magician's chamber'. In addition to his usual advisors, he had requested the presence of Master Brut and the Dean of St Asaph – Brut because his pleasant manner and gentle nature appealed to the female side of Owain's character, Dean Hywel because he wanted the church's reaction to a scheme he had in mind.

As was his custom, Rhys Gethin was the first to speak. Looking Owain straight in the eye, he said, 'We have proclaimed you Prince of Wales. Today we must march against Ruthin. The readiness is all.'

A rumble of approval rolled around the chamber. Owain smiled and shook his head.

He turned to Hywel and asked, 'Dean, am I correct in thinking that St Matthew's day falls on September 21st?'

'Yes Prince, you are correct.'

'And is it not true that the people of Ruthin hold a great fair on that day?'

Hywel nodded.

Owain continued, 'Today is the fifteenth day of the month. On the eighteenth the garrison of Ruthin will be in the middle of their preparations. That is the day we march against Ruthin. As a churchman you would have no objection to us taking advantage of our enemy's religiosity?'

Hywel coloured slightly and answered, 'I believe their observance of the festival has more to do with drinking and whoring than veneration of the saint. I have no objection.'

★

Owain Glyn Dŵr's army was mainly composed of bowmen and pikemen. Their body armour consisted of a metal cap and a quilted tunic, though a fortunate few sported a cuirass. In addition to the bow or pike each man carried a sword or an iron-headed cudgel. When they reached Ruthin, Lord Grey's men were caught completely off-guard and retreated within the castle walls, leaving the town undefended. Lord Grey stood on the battlements and showed no sign of issuing forth to give battle.

Owain turned in his saddle as Rhys Gethin rode up beside him, and exclaimed, 'We have no siege engines, neither have we the time to capture the castle.'

Rhys, his face lit up by a wicked smile, shouted, 'Leave the castle, let us burn the town around him while he stares impotently from his skunk hole.'

Owain remembered when, as a boy, he had visited the great fair at Ruthin. He saw again the glittering baubles, the streaming flags, the shining shields, the hobby horses, the tables of sweetmeats and the girls in their pretty dresses.

'Burn the market place. Burn all the houses,' Rhys urged again. 'Blacken the walls of his castle with the smoke from his burning town. He'll never live down the shame and we'll have sent a message to the other English settlements.'

Owain nodded his head reluctantly and, leaning across, laid a restraining hand on his captain's arm.

In a quiet, firm voice he said, 'Raze the town to the ground and slaughter all enemy soldiers who impede you, but spare all the women and children.'

For the next five days they devastated the settlements at Denbigh, Rhuddlan, Flint, Hawarden, Holt, Oswestry and Welshpool. There followed scenes of rejoicing in the rebel camp, but not all were pleased with their army's exploits.

Master Brut remarked wryly, 'All those houses burnt but not a castle taken.'

Owain's face darkened and he said, 'Not only not taken, not even attacked. For this rebellion to succeed, we must smash the castles that enshrine English authority in Wales, not destroy the homes of the peasants.'

Rhys intervened, 'This campaign has taught us one important lesson, our army must acquire siege equipment – towers, rams and catapults. We can construct towers 150 feet high covered with hides to protect the attackers from blazing arrows. It's not as if these weapons are a modern innovation. Dear God, Alexander used them against the Persians.'

That night, news reached Owain that a large force made up of levies from Shropshire, Staffordshire and Warwickshire, under the command of Hugh Burnell of Shrewsbury, was marching along the banks of the Severn with the intention of engaging them in battle and putting an end to their marauding.

That night Owain's dreams were troubled with doubts. He envisaged the battle scene with the two armies drawn up some thousand yards apart at either end of a long flat meadow – bordered on the left by a line of trees and on the right by the river. His men were stationed in two blocks with the bowmen placed between them in a wedge formation. In the distance, the enemy appeared as a huge amorphous mass. There then occurred the period of waiting, during which the soldiers in the front rank sat on the damp grass, drinking and eating. It had always amazed Owain how little dispute occurred in determining who stood in the front rank. By pushing forward, the grander and braver placed themselves before the humble and timid. During his years fighting in Richard's Scottish wars, Owain had often pondered on the nature of courage and had come to the conclusion that the truly noble expressed themselves through the terse idiom of courage.

The start of the battle was signalled when the sky was blotted out by a hail of arrows from the English archers. Owain woke with a cry as his vision was swamped by a sea of blood.

The following morning, it was with a troubled heart that Owain led his men onto the battle field and his mood darkened when he saw that Burnell's men vastly outnumbered his small force. Burnell's first arrow strike wrought carnage among the Welshmen and before they could strike back, the English soldiers charged and swept Owain's army from the field – some fleeing into the woods, others attempting to swim across the Severn. The defeat was catastrophic and taught Owain that his army was not capable of fighting a pitched battle and that the rebellion was over.

The brothers William and Rhys ap Tudor, cousins to Owain, had raised the flag of rebellion in Anglesey but were as swiftly repressed. King Henry was at Northampton when news reached him of the Welsh uprising. He immediately called for reinforcements and, marching westwards, made a complete circuit of north Wales before returning to Shrewsbury, where he issued a decree depriving Owain and the chief rebels of their landed property.

Gathering his family and adherents, Owain abandoned both Glyndyfrdwy and Sycharth, and retreated to an inaccessible, half-ruined fortress among the rocks and lakes of Snowdon. Using a swarm of stonemasons and carpenters, Owain converted the ruin into a spacious stronghold that could accommodate a large household together with a considerable number of well-armed men.

*

From the moment he entered the service of Owain Glyn Dŵr, Rhisiart became aware of Owain's young daughter Catherine. To say aware is an understatement – her innocent beauty possessed him. For Rhisiart, Catherine outshone the torches and tapers in the great hall at Glyndyfrdwy. She was the sun that illuminated his life. For her part, poor Rhisiart need not have existed – she ignored him.

Rhisiart was painfully conscious of his comparatively humble origins. His father was employed by the Sheriff of Hereford in a semi-legal role and his mother was a Norman. Rhisiart was a very distant cousin of Owain but even this tenuous connection was on the bastard side. He also knew that Owain was zealously guarding his daughter's virginity with the aim of her making an advantageous marriage that would further Owain's dynastic ambitions. However, the flight from Glyndyfrdwy was to provide Rhisiart with the opportunity to enter Catherine's cloistered world.

Before Owain retreated to his fortress in Snowdonia, he summoned Rhisiart and ordered him to take command of a small cavalry detachment and return to Glyndyfrdwy to rescue the garrison, together with the Arglwyddes and her ladies. Walter Brut, anxious for the well-being of his wife Alice, sought permission to join the squad and Owain readily gave his consent. It would be wrong to say that Rhisiart cut a heroic figure as he sat upon his big-boned black stallion. The horse, though large, moved with an extraordinarily clumsy gait that threatened to unhorse Rhisiart with every step the animal took. Rhisiart wore a coat of chain mail and a heavy crusader sword hung from his belt. The body armour and sword, though vigorously polished could not conceal their venerable ancestry. Beneath the peak of his metal cap, Rhisiart's hooked nose and piercing black eyes featured prominently.

When they reached Glyndyfrdwy, Rhisiart, leaving Walter to organise the garrison, ran up the stone steps to the second story. It was the first time he had ventured into the women's quarters and he was taken aback by the contrast with the austere hall below. He passed through what appeared to be a succession of heavily scented bowers festooned with cushions of every colour imaginable. He found the whole experience claustrophobic and was mightily relieved when he was confronted by the formidable figure of the Arglwyddes.

'You bring news of the battle?' she demanded.

'The battle was lost and I am here to escort you to Snowdonia where your lord awaits you. You are no longer safe here.'

The Arglwyddes flinched at Rhisiart's brutal message but responded bravely, 'Go and organise our transport while I gather my women. My husband has lost the first battle but he will win the war.'

Apart from Catherine who insisted on riding a horse, the Arglwyddes and her women were conveyed in two wagons. So it transpired that when they set out for Snowdonia, Rhisiart and Catherine rode together at the head of the column. This was the nearest Rhisiart had ever got to Catherine, and his heart thumped frantically beneath his chain mail.

Sensing his discomfiture, Catherine smiled mischievously and asked, 'What is the name of your magnificent black stallion?'

Rhisiart mumbled, 'Hercules.'

At that instant, Hercules stumbled and Rhisiart was nearly catapulted over his horse's head. As he hung desperately onto the reins, he heard Catherine's delighted laugh. Having resumed his upright posture and, in an attempt to retrieve his dignity, Rhisiart assured Catherine that as her protector he would sacrifice his life in her defence.

Catherine replied lightly, 'Much as I appreciate your commitment, I trust it will never be put to the test.'

Though the words were flippant, Catherine gazed at him with a newly awakened interest and as they rode on conversation between them flowed more easily.

The convoy and its escort had been travelling for about three hours when they saw up ahead a body of archers and pikemen, together with two horsemen.

Walter rode up alongside Rhisiart and said, 'See those on horseback.'

Rhisiart nodded.

Walter continued, 'The tall elegant one in black is the Lord of Nannau – a cousin of Owain Glyn Dŵr and his deadliest enemy. The other one, who looks like a gorilla, is David Gam. Two more fanatical lovers of the English would be hard to find.'

'We're in trouble then.'

The enemy archers had now spread across the road and raised their bows into the firing position.

Rhisiart spoke urgently, 'Form the men into a wedge with the wagons in the middle. We'll charge through them and then send the wagons on while we turn and block them.'

Nannau and Gam had now ridden up to within hailing distance.

'Your situation is hopeless,' Nannau cried. Then, with

an ugly smirk, he added, 'Surrender to us, we know how to treat the dependants of Owain Glyn Dŵr.'

David Gam, excitedly waving his arms, bellowed, 'Long live the House of Lancaster.'

Rhisiart responded, 'We'll never surrender to such a vile traitor as you, Lord Nannau.'

While this exchange was taking place, Catherine retreated to the wagons and Rhisiart's soldiers had formed a tight wedge around the wagons.

To the consternation of Nannau, Rhisiart raised his antique sword and shouted, 'Charge'.

Rhisiart saw the fear in the archers' eyes as the horsemen crashed into their fragile line and the wagons, with their escort of pikemen, rumbled over their squirming bodies. No sooner had the wagons broken through, than Rhisiart's men turned round and drove the demoralised enemy from the field. Rejoining the wagons, Rhisiart had a feeling that he would meet up with the Lord of Nannau one more time, and the encounter would be one engulfed in sorcery and horror.

CHAPTER 4

Death in the hollow of a tree

THE REST OF the journey to the Snowdonia fortress passed without further incident and, on entering the refuge, they found themselves in a world of breathtaking activity. The place swarmed with carpenters, stonemasons and armourers all frantically transforming the crumbling old ruin into a defensible stronghold.

Catherine had started out on the journey with scant knowledge or interest in Rhisiart but the manner in which he had guided and protected the convoy elicited her admiration and she studied him with a more kindly eye. His slightly hooked nose was not very prominent – almost Roman, she thought; and his black piercing eyes promised unbridled passion. Life in this primitive castle would, of necessity, be more informal than it had been in Glyndyfrdwy. Catherine would have ample opportunity to further her burgeoning relationship with Rhisiart.

Although confined within the walls of his mountain fastness, Owain was kept informed of developments throughout Wales by a network of faithful scouts. One evening, the proceedings in the great hall were interrupted by the entry of a messenger. Owain was conversing with his captain Rhys Gethin at the back of the hall.

Instead of seeking out Owain, the scout, who was obviously very excited, jumped on a table and addressed the whole assembly, 'Friends! The usurper Henry has created his son Hal, Prince of Wales.'

Owain's deep voice resonated from the back of the hall, 'I believe the people of Wales will have something to say about that. Am I dead? Is the crown without a head to rest on?'

A great cheer rose from the crowd and, to the rhythmic stamping of a thousand feet, the warriors chanted, 'Owain Glyn Dŵr, Prince of Wales; Owain Glyn Dŵr, Prince of Wales.'

The messenger raised his hand and cried, 'I have more news. Prince Hal has been stationed at Chester and given the task of maintaining an iron grip on north Wales.'

A derisory voice from the crowd cried, 'He's a greenhorn, inexperienced and of too tender years.'

The messenger retorted, 'A body of counsellors, headed by Henry Percy, the famous Hotspur, has been appointed to assist him. Hotspur, Justice of Chester and north Wales, sheriff of Flint, holder of Anglesey and Beaumaris, keeper of the lordship of Denbigh.'

Owain's voice again reverberated from the back of the hall. 'It is well to know who your enemy is. It will be against Hotspur that we next raise the banner of revolution.'

★

The next insurrection came sooner than Owain could have envisaged and he was not the instigator. The brothers William and Rhys ap Tudor, having been denied a pardon for their part in the earlier revolt, were now, together with forty followers, living as outlaws in the region around Conway. It was late March in the year 1401, William and Rhys were discussing their plight, as they sheltered from the wind and rain in a hovel in the forest.

'We were not brought up to live in conditions like this,' William whined.

Rhys, casting a look of contempt at William's miserable face, said sharply, 'Stop your moaning. You were the one who was all for joining Owain. Remember Owain has also lost his land and property.'

'Yes, but he is safely ensconced in his Snowdon bolthole while we wander the land like shipwrecked sailors.'

'Some way must be found to reverse our punishment.'

'You mean some way to make Prince Hal grant us a pardon?'

'Not Prince Hal, the real power lies with Hotspur. If we can capture Conway castle and hold it, we can dictate the terms of our pardon.'

'Capture Conway castle! You must be mad,' exclaimed William.

'I've studied the routine of the garrison. The castle does not have a church and the garrison attend the parish church outside the castle. Now, on Good Friday most of the garrison will be attending the service of tenebrae leaving the castle defended by very few soldiers. Our band of forty Welshmen will easily force the gate and establish themselves as the masters of the castle. The castle is strong and well provisioned and capable of withstanding a long siege. Hotspur will have to negotiate with us and we will be able to dictate our own terms.'

William's mood brightened and he intoned, 'Happy times are here again.'

Rhys admonished him, 'Do not celebrate too soon, brother. The enterprise is a hazardous one and the outcome uncertain.'

In the early hours of Good Friday, the castle, with its eight massive towers, loomed dauntingly out of the darkness. William and Rhys watched as practically the whole garrison emerged and, led by the constable John Massy, marched in good order to the parish church. When the last of their number entered the brightly lit church, Rhys heard the chanting of matins and lauds.

He summoned his men forward and addressed them urgently, 'The castle is now virtually undefended. I warrant the few men they've left are now carousing before the fire in great hall, totally convinced that no Welshmen would dare attack their impregnable fortress. Go forth silently and scale the gates, then the castle will be ours.'

By the time the priest had gradually extinguished the candles in the church as ritual demanded, Conway castle was in the hands of William and Rhys and their forty Welshmen. John Massy and his men, blissfully unaware of the disaster that had taken place, filed out of the church and marched briskly back to the castle. When they reached the gate, the constable was quickly made aware of the situation when he saw the Tudor brothers standing triumphantly on the battlements and heard their cries of derision.

Rhys called mockingly, 'Constable, scuttle to Prince Hal at Chester and explain how his mighty castle at Conway was captured by forty Welshmen and see how long it will take him to separate your head from your trunk.'

Realising the hopelessness of his position, Massy, with a few soldiers as escort, set out on the road to Chester. On entering Prince Hal's presence, Massy fell to his knees and falteringly admitted that the Welsh, in the form of the Tudor brothers and their adherents, had captured Conway castle. Prince Hal glanced helplessly around and seemed at a loss as to what he should do. He then asked Massy to narrate exactly what had happened. The poor man gave all the painful details of that Friday morning, including the fact that most of the garrison had been observing the service of tenebrae at the parish church.

Hotspur, who had been sitting by Hal's side, gave a great bellow and rose to his feet.

'Lost C-conway c-castle,' he shouted.

Hotspur was never sure what form his stutter would take from day to day. Some days he would have difficulty with the letter 'p', another day with 's'. Today it was evidently 'c'. He was however unabashed by this impediment and quite amused to find that most women found it quite attractive.

'Lost C-conway c-castle, to a handful of puny Welshmen,' he continued. 'C-conway c-castle, one of the six c-castles built by Edward I to secure his c-conquest of Wales. A c-castle of formidable defensive structure and daunting aspect. What's wrong with the English that we allow our religious faith to be exploited by the godless Welsh? First Owain attacks Ruthin while we prepare for the celebrations of St Mathew's day. Now those bastard Tudor brothers take C-conway c-castle while we sit like fools in church singing psalms and psalms and hymns.'

Hotspur's anger was understandable, he knew that he would be unable to quickly retake the castle. The walls were too strong to be breached and too tall to be scaled. In addition the garrison were provisioned to withstand a siege for many months. If he wanted a speedy resolution he would have to grit his teeth and negotiate with the Tudor brothers. This he did and, on condition that they vacated the castle, he granted them a full pardon and restored their lands and properties. This episode did not rebound to Hotspur's credit and opened up a rift between King Henry and Hotspur. Contrary to Rhys' prediction, Massy did not have his head separated from his trunk, but it was a damn close thing.

When news of the Tudor brothers' success reached Owain he smiled cynically and said, 'Now that they have achieved their object, we can expect no further support from them.'

★

When Owain had gathered together the remnants of his broken army, he ventured into the wilds of Plynlimon where he discovered a large enemy force encamped on the banks of the river Hyddgen. Owain, having learnt that the tactical sum of infantry and cavalry when carefully co-ordinated was far greater than the sum of the two parts when acting separately, now put this knowledge into practice. He attacked and routed the far larger force. This victory, against the odds, greatly enhanced Owain's reputation and men from all over Wales rallied to his support. So strong did he become that there was talk of him invading England.

The news of Owain's victory and its consequences so alarmed King Henry that he assembled a large army at Worcester and marched into south Wales, spreading destruction and slaughter wherever he went.

He established his headquarters at the abbey of Strata Florida, driving out the terrified monks at sword point and quartering his men and horses before the high altar. Henry exhibited his ruthless and cruel nature in the treatment of women and children, carrying them off as captives. Yet at the end of the campaign Henry had failed to even catch sight of Owain yet alone meet him in armed conflict, for Glyn Dŵr was far too wily to engage with an embattled royal army. A frustrated Henry was forced to withdraw his weary forces to England, his mission unaccomplished.

Hotspur left north Wales to command the Scottish border and, in his absence, Owain transferred his attention to north Wales. He attacked Prince Hal's train and carried the booty off to his Snowdon fortress. But an attack on the town and castle of Caernarvon failed disastrously, with the loss of three hundred men.

Thus the year 1401 ended in a stalemate.

★

It was a cold damp night in early February, when Owain received an unexpected caller at his Snowdon fortress. The visitor was the Dean of St Asaph, who came as an emissary of Hywel Sele, Baron of Nannau. A fire burned brightly in the centre of Owain's low ceilinged chamber. When Madoc ushered the dean into the room, Owain was staring out through one of the deep lancet windows cut in the thick outer wall.

Owain turned and said, 'Dean, you have found me in a good mood.'

'Indeed,' answered the Dean, cautiously.

'I have not long returned from a raid into Lord Grey's territory and am well pleased with booty I acquired. I have reached the stage when my need is not for more soldiers but for the gold to pay them.'

The dean smiled nervously and said, 'I come as a suppliant for your cousin Hywel Sele.'

'I had a feeling that was the case,' Owain retorted.

'Lord Nannau visited me. He feels the time has come to put an end to the vicious enmity that has marred the relationship between you. He proposes that you meet with him at his estate under the auspices of two high dignitaries of the cathedral. There to conclude a lasting truce that will prove of benefit to a future united Wales.'

'Very eloquently put, Dean. But you realise I must consult with my family and counsellors before I give you an answer. Madoc, escort the Dean of St Asaph to our guest quarters.'

A short while later, Owain's small chamber was crowded with his family and advisors, and the air rang with cries of dissent. The idea of Owain journeying to Nannau's territory to conclude a peace treaty with their arch enemy met with horrified disapproval.

Above the general hubbub the voice of the Arglwyddes

sounded deep and sonorous, 'That cursed man has nurtured in his bosom a jealousy of your pre-eminence, Owain. And I know that this offer of friendship is a perfidious contrivance to encompass your death. Once you set foot on his land, he will cut your throat.'

Owain's sons, Gruffydd and Maredudd, strongly supported their mother, crying out in unison, 'Father! Do not trust this man.'

Owain rose from his chair and in the manner of a teacher more than that of a warrior prince, reasoned with them, 'Our vision is of a Wales at peace with itself – a Wales under the rule of a prince who loves all of his subjects. How can I aspire to be that prince when there is within the royal household such a bitter feud as exists between Hywel Sele and myself? I must assume that the man is genuine. I must go and meet with him.'

The crowd fell silent, then the Arglwyddes spoke again, 'You must take Madoc with you.'

'No,' Maredudd cried out. 'I'm his son, I must accompany him.'

'I'm his eldest son,' Gruffydd shouted. 'It's my privilege to guard him.'

Owain said quietly, 'Rhisiart will be my squire.'

The Arglwyddes persisted, 'Madoc is a great warrior, Rhisiart a mere boy.'

Catherine protested, 'How can you say Rhisiart is a mere boy when you saw how his bravery saved us from Hywel Sele in the flight to Snowdon?'

Rhisiart smiled gratefully at Catherine who in turn blushed shyly.

Owain repeated firmly, 'Rhisiart will be my squire.'

★

The following morning Owain, Rhisiart and the Dean of Asaph set off over the frozen hills on their peace mission. Owain felt uncomfortably weighed down by the suit of chain armour, blessed by Iolo, that the Arglwyddes had insisted he wore. As they neared their destination, two grooms appeared out of the gloom and courteously informed Owain that they had been sent by their lord to conduct them safely to his castle. After a short while, Rhisiart turned in his saddle and discovered that the dean was no longer with them. Sensing treachery, he unsheathed his antique sword and held it in readiness at the side of his horse. He did not have to wait long. As they entered a clearing they found the tall, elegant figure of Hywel Sele sitting bolt upright with his longbow at the ready and pointing directly at Owain. Without a moment's hesitation, Owain spurred his horse towards Hywel Sele. Owain felt a heavy blow on his chest as the arrow struck home, but the chain mail held firm and the arrow failed to penetrate his flesh. The impact, however, knocked him backwards off his horse and he lay stunned on the ice hard floor of the clearing. The grooms, drawing their daggers, rode towards where Owain lay helpless, but Rhisiart waving his sword menacingly charged straight at them. Wisely deciding that their daggers were no match for Rhisiart's magnificent sword, the grooms turned tail and fled with Rhisiart in pursuit. Having driven them from the scene, Rhisiart now desperately wanted to return and rescue Owain, but, no matter how hard he tugged at Hercules' reins, the old horse, delighting in the chase, continued the pursuit.

Hywel Sele dismounted and walked to where Owain lay. Assuming that the arrow had killed him, Sele bent low over the body to gloat at the dead face of his detested cousin. Imagine his consternation when Owain, summoning strength from he knew not where, caught Hywel Sele with a blow to the side of the head from his armoured fist. The two men now grappled on the ground with a fury nurtured by years of intense hatred. Neither man could free his sword and so the struggle to the death became one of pure brute force. Owain grasped Sele around the waist and, with superhuman strength, staggered painfully to his feet. Driven by the wrath raging within him, Owain bent his adversary's body further and further back until he heard a sickening crack and felt Sele go slack in his arms. Owain realised that he had snapped the man's spine. Sele's head lolled on his shoulders but the movement in his eyes showed that he was still alive. Owain noticed, about a hundred yards away, a dead tree trunk. It was the height of a man and completely hollowed out – its black mouth stood out in stark contrast to the pure white snow surrounding it. He carried the living Sele over and hurled him into the hollow. At that moment Rhisiart returned, having reasserted control over Hercules.

He stared in horror at the figure in the tree trunk and muttered, 'But he's still alive. Aren't you going to dispatch him with a sword thrust?'

'No,' Owain said emphatically. 'Let him die there in the mouth of hell and reflect on his infamy.'

As they rode away, Sele's eyes followed them. Rhisiart, shocked by Owain's treatment of the dying man, shook his head and said, 'I never saw a man who looked so wistfully at the darkening sky.'

On the long journey back, Owain was disturbed by visions of Hywel Sele slowly and agonisingly dying in that hollow trunk. It caused him to question what had been the source of his passion and terrifying strength. Did it emanate from the faith of a Christian knight or did it spring from the evil inherent in the soul of a Welsh sorcerer who could summon spirits from the deep?

CHAPTER 5

The great comet

THERE WAS GREAT rejoicing when Owain and Rhisiart returned safely home and Catherine's eyes shone with pride as she learnt of Rhisiart's role in the adventure. Neither man divulged the fact that Owain had left the broken-backed Sele to suffer an agonising death in the hollow of a tree stump. There was much speculation as to the fate of the Dean of Asaph and whether he was complicit in the treacherous plot. All was revealed the next morning when a dishevelled and contrite dean appeared before the walls of the fortress and begged an audience with Lord Owain Glyn Dŵr. On entering Owain's presence, the dean fell on his knees.

'My Lord,' he cried. 'I was following some short distance behind you when I was abducted by Sele's men. I was only released when word came that Sele's plan had gone all amiss and he had been slain instead. Please forgive me for being the innocent dupe of an evil, devious man.'

Owain moved forward and helped Dean Asaph rise to his feet.

'Of course my old friend you were duped and there is nothing to forgive. You have arrived at a most opportune moment. The time when Wales will become a truly independent nation is at hand and I must plan its structure. One of the first institutions that will need reform is the church in Wales. To this end, I am forming a committee and it would please me greatly if you became a member.'

Rhisiart smiled, it amused him – the knack Owain had of restoring a bruised person's self-respect.

During the following months, Owain's position strengthened as support flowed in abundance to his stronghold on Snowdon. Henry Don of Kidwelly, a long-standing friend, sent word that he was ready to join Owain with an armed force whenever Owain raised the flag of rebellion once more. Messages of support arrived from Scotland and Ireland and it was rumoured that the Earl of Northumberland and his son Hotspur were mightily disillusioned with King Henry and were becoming more sympathetic to Owain's cause.

One balmy spring evening Owain and Walter Brut retired from the main hall where the men were relaxing and the Arglwyddes and her women were weaving a tapestry on the great loom. They settled in Owain's chamber and spoke earnestly of what the future held in store.

Brut said eagerly, 'Prince, you are doing for your people what Alfred the Great did for his.'

Owain stirred uneasily in his chair and replied, 'Alfred was a great commander whereas I am pleased to return from some squalid little raid with a dozen or so ponies loaded with plunder.'

'You will drive the English from our soil and then you will transform Wales as Alfred did England.'

'Alfred was not just a great military leader, he had the learning of a monk and founded universities. What do I know of universities?'

'That is where you are wrong, my Prince. Your knowledge of the scriptures and the occult is acknowledged throughout the land. You are the Welsh Alfred.'

Owain, visibly affected by Brut's blatant flattery, replied, 'Do you really think so? Where should I place this fledging seat of learning?'

'Not one! We must have two – one in the north, the other in the south.'

Owain laughed and said, 'Master Brut, that is so typical of you.'

★

One morning when Rhisiart and Owain were strolling in the courtyard, they were approached by Rhys Gethin and a soldier under escort.

Gethin saluted Owain and said curtly, 'This man has been arrested for spreading dissension among the ranks and attempting to desert.'

Owain viewed the short, thin creature held firmly by the two escorting soldiers. The man's position was desperate, for death was the normal punishment for desertion, but his demeanour was far from cringing.

'Your name,' Owain demanded.

A look of defiance passed across his clever, ferret like face as he answered, 'John ap Thomas, though what means a name like that to a great lord such as yourself. You lords! Who weaves the cloth of your garments? Who tills the soil and gathers in your harvests? And who die by the hundreds in your futile wars? I'll tell you who, the poor bloody peasants. You lords will do anything for the people except the one thing they crave.'

'And what is that?' asked Owain.

'Stop living like parasites off them. Get off their backs,' John barked.

'Considering your views on lords and gentlefolk, I'm surprised you're here supporting me.'

'I'm not here by choice, I assure you. I came with a contingent of fencible men from Powys – conscripted in other words.'

'We have here a true man of the people. John, you remind me of Wat Tyler, the leader of the Peasants' Revolt.'

'A man to admire and emulate.'

Shaking his head sadly, Owain asked, 'What is there to admire in a man who caused three days and nights of burning, looting, raping and slaughter in London, only to end up dead and with none of the peasants' grievances met or their hardship lightened?'

'Better to die gloriously in a lost cause than to live shamelessly under injustice and oppression.'

'No, no, my friend! There is a better way to improve the lot of the people. I am fighting for a Wales free from English oppression; a Wales with its own prince, parliament, chancery, church, and judiciary; a Wales with its own universities, independent of Oxford and Cambridge. When I rule such a Wales, I promise you that I will set up a parliament to which I will summon four men from every commute in Wales. These men will not be drawn from the elite but will be good, honest citizens like yourself.'

Rhisiart wondered how Owain's determination to rule Wales could coexist with a democratic parliament. English kings considered parliament to be a confounded nuisance and summoned it as infrequently as possible. John, however, had no such doubts and stepping forward he grasped Owain's hands.

'A parliament, composed of such people, would make Wales the envy of the nations of the world,' John cried. 'Honour that promise and I'm your man for life.'

Gethin now intervened. 'My Lord Glyn Dŵr, if you're not going to hang him for desertion, I wish to make it clear my men do not want him back as a comrade.'

'I understand their feelings. Henry Don of Kidwelly, one of my staunchest allies, is on his way here with an armed force. Assign John ap Thomas to his command.' Then turning to John, he said, with a wry smile, 'Serve him well, for he is a noble gentleman.'

★

The garrison had barely risen from sleep when there came a frenzied hammering on the door of the great hall. As soon as Rhisiart had drawn back the massive bolts, Father Huw pushed his way into the hall and confronted the bemused household.

Father Huw, his voice hoarse with excitement, cried, 'All night long have I prayed on my knees outside these walls for God to give us a sign. And now my prayers have been answered. Follow me out and see how the angels of God stream across the heavens in support of our Prince, Owain Glyn Dŵr.'

Staring up at the sky, all were astounded to see a blazing ball of fire, with a long trail of fierce flames, majestically traversing the firmament.

Among the excited babble, one uncouth wag observed, 'It's a gob of divine spume on its way to a heavenly spittoon.'

He was angrily shouted down.

Walter Brut was the first to make a considered judgement. 'Well Father, I don't know about a host of angels but I do know that this flying object is a comet, and is made up of ice, dust and gas. I also know that there have been two comets in the past and that each of them portended a great historical event – the birth of Christ and the rise to power of Uther Pendragon. So who knows what this phenomenon might herald?'

Owain's face was inscrutable and he said nothing.

That night in the great hall, Iolo sang a ballad he had written to celebrate the appearance of the comet.

The first great comet,
the star of Bethlehem,
heralded the birth of Christ
and the salvation of man.

The second great comet
proclaimed the power
of Uther Pendragon
and Arthur his son.

The third great comet,
as it blazes high
in the northern sky,
presages the triumph
of Owain Glyn Dŵr.

In mid-April, quite by chance, Owain received intelligence that Reginald Grey was at Ruthin. Owain, with a large body of men feigned an attack on the castle. On a prearranged signal, the major part of Owain's army fled, leaving Owain and his housecarls, including Rhisiart, Madoc, Gethin, Brut and his sons Gruffydd and Maredudd, apparently abandoned. The temptation proved too strong for Grey to resist and he left the safety of his castle to capture Owain. As soon as Grey and his men sallied forth, Owain's men returned in overwhelming numbers and Grey was captured. Securely fettered, Grey was thrown on a horse and carried in triumph to Owain's Snowdon fortress.

The entire household was assembled on the ramparts when Owain and his warriors returned in triumph to his Snowdon lair. In her eagerness to see if Rhisiart was among the returning heroes, Catherine stood on tiptoe. Since Rhisiart's departure, her dreams had been riven with images of Rhisiart, broken limbed, lying in a pool of blood with no one to give him succour. She stood like Criseyde on the walls of Troy eagerly watching the defenders of the city return from battle and desperately hoping to see her lover Troilus in their number.

Catherine mouthed silently, 'There is my father, how magnificent he looks with his banner emblazoned with the lion rampant of Mathrafal. And there is my Rhisiart! How nobly he rides beside my father. How sternly his dark eyes flash under the peak of his helmet.'

When the cavalcade entered the courtyard, Catherine flew down the steps and ran to Rhisiart to help him dismount. Owain observed the affection with which his daughter laid her hands around Rhisiart's shoulders.

'I must nip this in the bud,' he thought. 'Rhisiart is a good man but Catherine is destined for greater things.'

Brut's wife, Alice, moved purposefully to where Lord Grey, astride a horse and with his arms pinioned behind his back, cut a sorry figure. His long, pale, atavistic face was frozen into a mask of despair. Alice, her slender body sheathed in a tight fitting gown of green silk, stared in contempt at the humiliated man and spat fully into his face.

Owain, thoroughly disconcerted by Alice's action, barked, 'Why was that man left unattended? Take him to the cells and see that he is fettered securely to the wall. Rhisiart, you superintend the operation. His ransom will fill our coffers.'

Alice, shaking with rage, stood rooted to the spot. Owain was unable to take his eyes off her. He remembered that there had been rumours that Brut's wife had been abducted by Grey's men and molested before being released. This would explain her behaviour now and the dignified frigidity she had exhibited since joining them. Gazing at Alice, there came into his mind a vision of her, encased in shining golden armour and riding a white charger, leading his men into battle. He saw her not as a desirable young woman but as the symbol of a resurgent Wales.

Owain shook his head and muttered under his breath, 'Banish such fantastical thoughts. There is an enemy to defeat and a kingdom to be won.'

★

The extent to which Owain's exploits had increased his reputation was manifested when his old friend Henry Don of Kidwelly arrived at Snowdon with two hundred men, made up of cavalry and infantry, and a stack of gold. Rhisiart, who had never met Henry Don but had heard much about him from Owain, had imagined him to be a man of ample proportions. Even his name evoked a sense of great bulk. It therefore came as a great surprise that, when Owain introduced him to Henry Don, Rhisiart found himself confronted by a dark-haired little man with a neatly pointed beard.

'He looks more like a scholar than a soldier,' thought Rhisiart.

'What function do you perform in Owain's entourage,' Henry Don asked, in a soft but deep voice.

'I am his secretary and squire, my Lord Kidwelly,' Rhisiart answered nervously.

'Not Lord Kidwelly,' Henry Don said sternly. 'Plain Master Henry Don of Kidwelly.'

Owain gave an amused snort and called for John ap Thomas. Rhys Gethin pushed John forward.

'I give this fine fellow to you as a gift,' Owain said to Henry Don. 'On being given the choice of being hanged for attempted desertion or remaining faithful to our cause, he chose not to be hanged.' On seeing the dubious glance Henry Don directed at John ap Thomas, Owain continued, 'Oh! You can trust him. He is a great champion of the peasants, a latter-day Wat Tyler.'

John intervened eagerly, 'I'll gladly follow a man who scorns the title Lord for that of Master.'

'Then that's settled,' said Henry Don.

★

The district of Maelienydd formed part of the extensive border territories of the ancient house of Mortimer. The heir was a boy of ten, Edmund Mortimer, whom King Henry kept in close custody, because the lad, by the rules of lineal descent, had a greater claim to the throne than the King himself. In the absence of the boy, his uncle, a young man twenty-five years of age and also called Edmund, ruled the Mortimer lands in his place.

Owain's success in Ruthin caused panic in the English parliament and King Henry recalled Hotspur to his old post of royal lieutenant in north Wales. An opportunist to his fingertips, Owain decided to switch his attack to the mountains of Maelienydd.

In the council of war that preceded the attack, Owain attempted to define their objectives and the strategy to achieve them.

Rhys Gethin, the grizzled veteran of many such campaigns, disagreed. 'Prince, the setting down of objectives and the drawing up of plans are a waste of time when we have no idea how the enemy will react. We should blaze a trail through the heart of Mortimer's territory and when we see his reaction then will be the time to worry about strategy.'

Owain sensed that the majority of the council were with Rhys Gethin and conceded gracefully. 'We will follow the advice of my captain and wait to see the nature of Mortimer's retaliation.'

A fleeting smile of gratification softened Rhys Gethin's rugged countenance.

To reassert his authority, Owain turned to Henry Don and said, 'I will march on foot with the infantry while your cavalry will protect both our flanks and send scouting parties forward to seek news of the enemy.'

Anxious to smooth Owain's ruffled feathers, Rhys Gethin proclaimed loudly, 'An excellent tactical ploy...'

Owain silenced him with a withering glance.

When the members dispersed, Owain asked his sons, Gruffydd and Maredudd, to remain behind.

His sons, expecting their father to give them further instructions concerning the coming affray, were shocked when he said, 'Sons, I order you to stay here with my brother Morgan and guard my mountain Llys.'

Ignoring their outraged protests, he continued, 'All the people most precious in my life lie here. I entrust them to your care.'

When they persisted in their dissent, Owain said in a dangerously quiet voice, 'This is not a request, it is an order.'

★

The long march into Maelienydd was an exhausting affair in the heat of midsummer and the men welcomed the cool of night when they gathered around the bivouac fires to cook their meals and sleep. During the march Rhisiart and Walter Brut found themselves together and such was the affinity that Rhisiart felt for the Lollard that he soon confided in Brut his passion for Catherine.

Walter listened sympathetically to the young man's tale, then said gently, 'You know, Rhisiart, not all love stories have a happy ending. I'm thinking of Abelard and Héloise, and in particular of Troilus and Criseyde. Their mutual love promised to be eternal but she soon gave herself to another.'

'Catherine is no wanton,' Rhisiart cried. 'She would never love another.'

'I'm sure you are right. Perhaps Abelard and Héloise is a more apt precedent as their idyll was destroyed by Héloise's uncle, who had poor Abelard castrated.'

Rhisiart winced and said, 'But who would wish to put an end to our relationship?'

'Daughters are useful pawns for ambitious barons. Catherine might love you but her father, to enhance his dynastic ambition, will marry her off to some noble regardless of her wishes. Such is the way of princes in this grasping world.'

For the remainder of the day, Rhisiart, greatly perturbed by Walter's words, marched on in silence.

It was late afternoon on June 21st, when Owain's forces arrived at the village of Pilleth, where Henry Don, having returned from a scouting foray, had important news for Owain.

'Prince, my scouts report that Edmund Mortimer has marched out of Ludlow at the head of a large army of tenants and supporters, and is moving west along the bank of the river Lugg.'

'You say, a large army — how many men?' asked Owain.

'I'd estimate 2,000, including a large contingent of Welsh archers.'

Owain turned to Rhys Gethin and said, with a laugh, 'Time now to plan a strategy, my Captain?'

Rhys Gethin grunted his approval.

Owain spoke with authority, 'I know this area well. The village church lies at the foot of a steep hill, Bryn Glas. We will establish ourselves on the brow of that hill and destroy the enemy as they attempt to advance up the hill.'

John ap Thomas, standing with Henry Don's men,

muttered under his breath, 'I hope this strategy will prove more successful than it did for King Harold at Hastings.'

Owain heard him and replied, 'Ah! John the sceptic, if everyone obeys orders and no one gets tempted down the slope, it will.'

At this moment a soldier pushed his way forward. He was dragging a terrified wretch, bound tightly with ropes.

'My Prince, I caught this villain spying on our camp. He's Welsh and, to his eternal shame, one of Mortimer's men.'

'String him up and let him dance on the air,' Rhys Gethin demanded.

The prisoner fell to his knees and pleaded with Owain, 'My Lord, I and hundreds of fellow Welshmen were conscripted into Mortimer's army against our will. If you release me, I'll go back and incite my fellow Welshmen to change sides during the battle.'

Rhys Gethin snorted and said, 'A likely story, this fellow persuading hundreds to change their allegiance.'

The prisoner responded eagerly, 'It will be easier than you imagine. The men are near revolt already. Burdened by the new repressive laws against the Welsh and fired by an enthusiasm for the national cause, it will take little to change their allegiance.'

'Enough! The man's a spy,' cried Rhys Gethin. 'Bring a rope and find a tree with a stout bough.'

Walter Brut now stepped forward and addressed Owain, 'My Prince, imagine the devastation caused to the enemy if hundreds of their own archers turn their arrows on their leaders. Such an occurrence is to be devoutly prayed for. Even if this man is a spy, what do we lose by releasing him?'

Rhys Gethin replied, 'He'll go straight to Mortimer and reveal our position.'

Walter Brut walked up to Rhys Gethin and whispered in his ear, 'But we'll be ready at the top of the hill waiting for him. That is exactly what we want.'

Rhys Gethin shrugged his shoulders and turned his back on Walter.

Owain ordered, 'Release him. This is a chance we must take.' Then staring hard at the prisoner, he said, 'I am giving you the opportunity to strike a blow for the Welsh nation that will reverberate throughout the land, even down to the parliament at Westminster.'

That night Owain's forces ascended the steep slope of Bryn Glas and established their defences on the summit. Henry Don's cavalry dismounted and tethered their horses behind the hill. All they could do now was wait for the dawn of St Alban's day. Mortimer's forces spent the night at nearby Whitton and arrived at the foot of Bryn Glas at daybreak. Their measured tread shook the ground and the valley echoed to the rhythmic beat of their stamping feet. They then, in full battle gear, attempted to climb the steep slope in the teeth of a persistent barrage of arrows. Valiantly they struggled upward as if into a hailstorm, their shoulders hunched and heads bowed. As they neared the top they were slaughtered in savage, close order combat. The air resounded with the clash of steel on steel and the cries of distress and pain. The mountain stream ran red with blood. The end came suddenly when Mortimer's Welsh archers switched allegiance and directed their arrows on their own men. Walter Brut turned to Rhisiart, who was fighting at his side, and smiled in triumph.

'Our prisoner did not let us down,' he shouted.

Mortimer had led his army to a disastrous defeat and the

corpses of 800 of his men lay on the slope, soaked in their own blood. His humiliation did not, however, end there. In the final stages of the battle he was captured and brought before Owain.

Owain eyed the elegant, pale-faced youth and muttered, 'So Henry sends against me a foppish courtier but newly released from his mother's apron strings.'

Mortimer replied angrily, 'Sir, you do me and my noble family wrong. The men who died so bravely this day were led by a scion of a great warrior family – a family that has faithfully served the kings of this nation from time immemorial.'

'What you lack in military acumen you make up for in the eloquence of your speech,' Owain said dryly.

'Then let my eloquence move you to allow the English to remove their dead from the battlefield where they are an abomination to God.'

'Never! Their rotting carcasses will be a memorial to my resounding victory.'

Owain then turned his back on Mortimer and walked swiftly away.

That night as Walter Brut and Rhisiart stood guard, they were conscious of the charnel house atmosphere that surrounded them.

Walter Brut whispered, as if not to disturb the dead, 'I've heard it said that at the time of Edmund Mortimer's birth at Ludlow, the grooms found all the horses in his father's stables bathed in blood to their fetlocks. It was taken as an augury that the child's destiny would also be bathed in blood.'

Rhisiart answered, 'Well that is certainly true this day. I pity the poor fellow that he is cursed in that way.'

Later that night the two friends heard a chilling rustling

sound coming from the corpses that littered the slope. They then observed black shadowy figures bent low scurrying furtively over the dead bodies like rats.

Rhisiart started out to investigate but Walter laid a restraining hand on his shoulder and said, 'Don't venture out there in the dark, wait until the light of day.'

The following morning, Rhisiart and Walter discovered that during the night the Welsh women accompanying Owain's army had obscenely mutilated the bodies of the fallen.

CHAPTER 6

The death of Hotspur

I N THE PALACE at Westminster, a querulous King Henry was in heated conversation with Worcester, Northumberland and Hotspur; the bone of contention being Hotspur's refusal to hand over to Henry a number of Scottish nobles that Hotspur had captured during his campaign on the border.

'I have been too temperate in dealing with these indignities,' Henry complained.

Hotspur was quick to answer, 'My liege, I did deny no p-prisoners. As I recall, when the fighting was done and we stood in triumph on the top of Homildon Hill, some p-popinjay, demanded that I hand over my captives. I was weak with my exertions and bleeding from my wounds. It made me mad to see him so fresh and smell so sweet amid all the blood and spilt guts, so I dismissed him with a curse.'

Northumberland added eagerly, 'Your Majesty, do not impeach what he said then, so he may unsay it now.'

'P-pay Mortimer's ransom and you can have my p-prisoners,' Hotspur challenged Henry.

Worcester came forward and said, 'The noble Mortimer, leading the men of Herefordshire to fight against the wild and irregular Glendower, was taken captive by the rude hand of that Welshman, and a thousand of his people butchered.'

'Yes, that I know,' Henry said impatiently. 'I also know that those Welsh women who followed Glendower's army inflicted such vile misuse on the bodies of the dead that it cannot be spoken of without great shame. Foolish Mortimer, who has wilfully betrayed the lives of those that he led to fight against that great magician Glendower. Let no man ask me for one penny cost to ransom home that traitor Mortimer.'

Hotspur, incensed, cried, 'A traitor! Mortimer a traitor? Never did a man fight so nobly for his sovereign liege. Let no man, king or commoner slander him with the word traitor.'

Henry, his voice shaking with rage, said, 'Northumberland, curb that insolent puppy of a son, and order him to send his prisoners to us or you will hear more of this. As for Mortimer, he can rot in Glendower's mountain fastness before I pay ransom.'

Henry, with a dismissive wave of the hand, indicated that their presence was no longer welcome.

Out in the courtyard, Hotspur, drunk with choler, cried, 'If the devil comes and roars for them, I'll not send them to that usurping scoundrel.'

Northumberland said quietly, 'Remember, my son, we helped to put him on the throne.'

'Allegiances can change,' Hotspur retorted.

★

On returning to Snowdonia, Owain reviewed his position and came to the conclusion that it was one of considerable advantage. King Henry was so beset with possible trouble from the French and Scots that the English in the Marches were barely able to maintain themselves in their walled towns and castles and all thought of taking the offensive against the Welsh had been abandoned. This meant that he was able to move his headquarters back to Glyndyfrdwy.

There was one thing that exercised his mind – what should he do about Edmund Mortimer? At present the unfortunate young man was confined in a prison cell but was unfettered and being treated humanely. Over the last few months, Owain had come to rely on Walter Brut's judgement. He decided to consult Walter, he respected the Lollard for his clear thinking and his humanity.

Walter answered Owain unhesitatingly, 'You faced the same problem with Grey. Should you satisfy the bloodlust of your men and hang the man or increase your war chest by offering him for ransom? You were shrewd enough then to make the right choice, why prevaricate now?'

'The choice is not the same. I have no intention of hanging the poor lad. Should I ransom him or try to form an alliance with the Mortimer family? There are rumours of a rift between the Mortimers and the King.'

'Offer him for ransom. If the King pays it, you'll know the rumours are false. If he refuses, the rumours are correct.'

Through emissaries, Owain informed Henry of the ransom required to free Mortimer, and waited for a reply. After several months it became evident that Henry had no intention of paying the ransom. It suited him to have Edmund Mortimer incarcerated at a time when the Percy family were threatening revolt.

The situation gave Owain an opportunity to attempt to form a tripartite alliance between the Welsh, the Percys and the Mortimers.

When Owain entered Edmund's cell, the young man sprang to his feet and asked eagerly, 'Word yet of my ransom?'

Owain shook his head and, feigning concern, said, 'From Henry, not a word. From others, I learn that, such is his mistrust of your family, he is happy to have you in captivity here. Reconcile yourself to being my guest for many more years.'

Edmund buried his head in his hands and cried out, 'Many more years confined in this one room. I'll dash my head against its cruel stone walls before I submit to that.'

Owain laid a consoling hand on Edmund's shoulder and said, 'I think it is time to make your stay here more congenial. I will give you the run of the castle and treat you as my son, subject, of course, to you swearing an oath that you will not attempt to escape.'

When Owain left the cell, he was not alone, Edmund walked beside him. Owain, a smile of quiet satisfaction playing around his lips, placed a fatherly arm around the neck of the unsuspecting young man.

The game was now afoot and Owain's next move was to inform Catherine that he expected her to show compassion and kindness towards their unfortunate prisoner. Catherine, with a toss of her pretty head, replied that the man meant nothing to her and that she expected their meetings would be infrequent and brief, so any expressions of compassion and kindness would have to come from others. Owain's reaction startled and frightened her.

His face slowly turned crimson and in a voice as sharp as the blade of Madoc's axe, he said, 'You are the daughter of a prince and will obey without demur the orders of that prince. Use your womanly charms to become his constant companion and make him look favourably on the Glyn Dŵr family.'

At these words, Catherine saw clearly her father's intent and her blood ran cold.

'Father, my heart and mind are set on Rhisiart in so wondrous a manner that all the world could not unbind my love, nor cast Rhisiart's presence out of my heart.'

Owain said sadly, 'Catherine, those of noble stock can never enjoy the freedom to love whom they may. When they marry it is to found alliances and forge new kingdoms.' He then ordered sternly, 'Forget Rhisiart and cease your dalliances with him. He is no man of substance in this power game. Edmund Mortimer is the man for you.'

An unhealthy paleness spread over Catherine's tear-stained face and she answered, 'I will obey you father, as I must. But know that, from this day, I care not whether you live or in the cold earth lie.'

★

Owain was a man who, once he started a task, could not rest until it was completed. He summoned Rhisiart to his study and briskly informed him that Catherine would no longer welcome his attentions as her interest was engaged elsewhere. Rhisiart realised immediately what 'elsewhere' meant and that Catherine was acting under duress. This was part of Owain's strategy to form an alliance with the powerful Mortimer clan.

In his heart he acknowledged that the stakes were so high in this game of politics, that the love which bound Catherine and him together counted for nothing in the annals of history.

Crushed, Rhisiart sought consolation from his friend the Lollard. Walter listened sympathetically as Rhisiart concluded his tale of woe with the words, 'I am lost, for all things happen through necessity. To be forlorn must be my destiny.'

Walter responded, 'There are great scholars who claim that fate rules all and they can prove it so. But others, equally learned, will say their arguments are weak and free will is the truth.'

'Whom to believe I do not know.'

'God knows all and cannot be mistaken. Things must fall as providence foresaw. We must face the fact, if God foretells our every word and deed, there's no free will whatever scholars plead.'

'So it is by God's will that I have been denied fair Catherine. Since God sees everything and orders all things by his own design, a man's destiny has been preordained. May mine be a swift death.'

Walter said urgently, 'Whoever saw a man so distressed? Have you not lived happily for many years without Catherine? Were you born merely to please her? Think more sensibly, love is but a disease. In love, new pleasures will come and go.'

Rhisiart watched, with an ache in his heart, the developing relationship between Catherine and Edmund. He noted the sadness etched on Catherine's pale face and the look of stony indifference she cast upon her father. Inevitably, and to Owain's satisfaction, arrangements were set in hand for the marriage of the two young people. Rhisiart was given the galling task of writing letters to every enemy of the House of Lancaster informing them of the pending alliance between Owain Glyn Dŵr and the Mortimer family.

The relationship between Rhisiart and Owain was further strained by the arrival at Glyndyfrdwy of a tall, thin young man with a pair of spectacles perched precariously on the end of his aquiline nose. Dr Griffith Young was an exceptionally able cleric and a doctor of canon law who had tried to progress within the church but had been thwarted by his humble birth and the fact that he was Welsh. It was therefore not surprising that he joined the flood of clerics and notable people joining Owain's revolt. Owain very quickly noted the cleric's talent and made Young his chancellor, a position that Rhisiart had been hoping to fill.

During the weeks before the marriage, Mortimer, a Norman gentleman to his fingertips, treated Catherine with gentleness and courtly dignity. This comforted Catherine and she came to spend more of her time with him than with any other member of the household. The Arglwyddes was in charge of the preparations for the ceremony and a magnificent occasion it turned out to be – from the vast rainproof pavilion to the details of Catherine's flowing white gown. Owain was resplendent in a cloak of scarlet while Rhisiart, in keeping with his wretched mood, wore a costume of direst black relieved by flashings of silver. Rhisiart, together with Walter Brut and Griffith Young, stood in the front row of spectators waiting for the bridal procession to emerge from the chapel and make its way to the pavilion. To Rhisiart's annoyance, Young talked excitedly about the political significance of the marriage.

'Sir Edmund Mortimer is a brother-in-law of Hotspur,' he announced. 'And so this union will make Lady Catherine a sister-in-law to the mighty warrior. This marriage could not have come at a better time. It is rumoured that Hotspur is on the verge of raising the great Percy standard against the King.'

'You talk only of the political implications and ignore the devastation caused to the individuals involved,' Rhisiart rejoined.

At that moment Edmund and a pale faced Catherine stepped out of the chapel porch. As they passed Rhisiart, Catherine stopped for an instant and whispered in his ear, 'The first born I will name Rhisiart.'

That night in the bridal bed, Edmund behaved with such understanding and tenderness, that Catherine resolved that, though Rhisiart would always reign in her heart, she would be a faithful and compliant wife to Edmund.

★

Hotspur was pacing the floor of a room in his castle at Warkworth, studying the contents of a letter he had recently received. When his wife Elizabeth appeared, he hastily pushed the missive into a pocket of his tunic and said, 'Kate, I must leave w-within two hours.'

Elizabeth responded sharply, 'It will make little difference to me whether you are here or not. For three weeks you have lain by my side in our bed like a wooden effigy and not touched my naked body, though I longed for the feel of your lusty limbs entwined with mine. You have lost the blood from your cheeks and stalk the corridors of this dwelling ignoring me and muttering of prisoners' ransom, plots, bloodshed and battles yet to come. What is it that carries you away?'

'W-why my horse, Kate, my horse.'

'Cease your fooling, and I wish you would stop calling me Kate when you know full well my name is Elizabeth.'

'Elizabeth? No, far too austere for a spirited lass like you.'

'I fear my brother Mortimer has sent for you to assist him in some treasonable enterprise against the King.'

'I love you infinitely, but you must question me no more. W-where I go, there shall you go too. Today I set forth, tomorrow you. W-will this content you, Lady Henry Percy?'

'No, it does not content me, but I must obey.'

★

Hotspur's secret destination when he rode from Warkworth castle was the archdeacon's house in Bangor. When he arrived he found assembled Worcester, Edmund Mortimer and Owain Glyn Dŵr. Owain assumed the role of chairman, as if by divine right, and bade them to take their seats.

Owain looked keenly at Hotspur and remarked, 'I've

heard it said that whenever the King speaks of Hotspur his cheeks turn pale and he wishes you in heaven.'

Hotspur retorted, 'And you in hell.'

Owain sensed that Hotspur was out to mock him and he decided to answer in kind.

'As well he might,' Owain responded. 'At my birth, the heavens were all on fire and the earth trembled.'

'The earth shook to see the heavens on fire, and not in fear of your nativity.'

Edmund now intervened, 'Peace, brother-in-law, you provoke our esteemed host.'

Mischievously, Owain claimed, 'I can call spirits from the vasty deep.'

'But will they c-come?' Hotspur retorted.

Owain laughed and said, 'Enough of this banter, I know you English call me the Devil's disciple. Let's to the business in hand.'

After detailed discussion, Hotspur summarised their plan of action, 'Edmund, you will, without delay, write to your former associates on the Hereford border informing them of your change of allegiance. This will serve as a declaration of war. Tomorrow, my uncle Worcester and I will ride to Chester and raise the flag of rebellion. We will then set forth for Shrewsbury to join my father and the Scottish lord, Douglas. You, Glendower, are not yet in a position to help us.'

'No, my forces are heavily engaged in Carmarthenshire and it will take me a fortnight to withdraw them and regroup. Then I will join you.'

Hotspur looked quizzically at Owain's enigmatic countenance and an ugly thought entered his mind – was Glendower prevaricating? In a fortnight the outcome of the battle with King Henry would be known, leaving Glendower free to choose his course of action.

In early July, Hotspur publicly renounced the allegiance of the Percy family to King Henry and charged him with perjury based on his claim to the throne, imprisoning and murdering King Richard II and not permitting free Parliamentary elections. He and Worcester, with an army of 10,000 men marched south to Shrewsbury.

Henry, who was hastening north to the Scottish border, heard of Hotspur's defection and immediately changed direction and, with an army of 15,000 men, marched west to intercept Hotspur before the gates of Shrewsbury. The two armies arrived at the town on July 20th, 1403. Hotspur set up camp on the north and Henry on the south of the river Severn. The following morning the King's forces crossed the river at Uffington and took up a position on the open ground of the floodplain. The scene was set for a bloody confrontation.

★

Hotspur stared gloomily at the army confronting him and said to Douglas, 'Henry has ch-chosen well, in this open ground he c-can make better use of his larger numbers.'

Douglas replied, 'When the good Northumberland, your father, arrives with his force, we will no longer be outnumbered.'

'What worries me is, that if you arrived on time, why is he so tardy?'

Worcester, attempting to dispel the gloom, said, 'Fear not, Hotspur, your father is as constant as the North Star. He will be here at our side before the battle.'

'Then, by God, he's c-cutting it fine,' retorted Hotspur.

A travel-stained messenger rushed up to Hotspur and, with the words, 'My Lord, a letter from your father,' thrust the missive into his hand.

'A letter?' exclaimed Hotspur. 'Of what use is a letter from him? Why is he not here himself?'

'He cannot come, my Lord, for he is grievous ill.'

'How has he the leisure to be sick at such a c-critical time? Tell me, who leads the men he has sent?'

'He has sent no power.'

'Sent no power! What is in his mind?'

'His letter bears his mind, not I, my Lord.'

Hotspur tore open the letter and avidly read the text.

'He writes that sickness has prevented him leading his army and that no other would take the responsibility. But he urges us to c-continue in our enterprise and see how fortune is disposed to us.'

Worcester shook his head and said, 'Your father's sickness is a grievous blow to us.'

'A blow! It is a perilous gash. It is as if a very limb were lopped off,' cried Hotspur. 'Yet, I will throw off the fear of defeat and death and will hazard all.'

Douglas bellowed, 'Bravo! There is not such a word spoke in Scotland as this term of fear.'

'My father and Glendower being both away, the greater the renown if we carry the day.'

Between the two encamped armies, King Henry and Prince Hal parleyed with Hotspur and Worcester to no effect. Hotspur rejected any terms and Worcester traded insults with the King. The negotiations finished at noon and the protagonists returned to their armies. The King raised his mace and the battle commenced. Immediately the sky turned black as the archers launched a deadly hail of arrows. Hotspur's bowmen proved superior, killing most of the royal vanguard. Henry watched in alarm as his men fell like leaves in autumn. Prince Hal, who was standing on the front line, received an arrow fully in the face and suffered a deep and terrible wound. He was carried to the rear where he was attended to by the physician general. He then, despite the pleas of the surgeon, insisted on returning to the fray. The battle had now degenerated into a mêlée of hand-to-hand combat and Henry's superior numbers began to tell. In a desperate attempt to turn the tide, Hotspur led a cavalry charge against the tight group of housecarls around Henry. He succeeded in killing the carrier of the royal standard but the King escaped. Hotspur now scoured the battlefield in a desperate search to find and slay Henry. To improve his vision, he raised his visor for an instant. An alert royal archer recognised his coat-of-arms and sped an arrow through the aperture and deep into Hotspur's brain. Their leader killed, the rebels fled.

As dusk fell, Henry and Prince Hal stood at the entrance to their tent looking out over the battlefield.

Prince Hal said softly, 'Father, one cannot see the good earth for the bodies of the dead that lie upon it.'

Henry replied, 'Thousands died in only a few hours and, despite our victory, we lost more men than the rebels.'

Hotspur's butchered body was carried in and placed at their feet.

Hal, mimicking Hotspur's stammer, said to the bloodied corpse, 'Percy, you are food for w-worms.'

Henry said, thoughtfully, 'When that body contained a spirit, a kingdom was too small for it, but now two paces of the vilest earth is room enough.'

'Worcester and that Scot, Douglas, are among the prisoners.'

'See that Worcester be tried for treason, convicted and executed. As for that Scot, he fought well today. Hold him for ransom.'

'What now, Father?'

'You and I will towards Wales, to fight with Glendower. Rebellion in this land must lose its sway.'

CHAPTER 7

The tide turns

N ORTHUMBERLAND, TOGETHER WITH his wife and daughter-in-law, was walking in the orchard of Warkworth castle. The earl, though he appeared to have recovered from the illness that had confined him to his bed, was in a vexatious mood.

'I curse pernicious rumour,' he muttered, 'that stuffs men's minds with false reports. First it proclaims the King is slain and Hotspur has won the day. Then it whispers, Hotspur's bloodied corpse lies at the feet of the victorious King.'

Elizabeth said bitterly, 'Had you been at your son's side instead of sulking in your bed, you would have known the outcome before now.'

Lady Northumberland rebuked Elizabeth, 'That was uncalled-for and cruel.'

Before the women could continue their altercation, Travers, a faithful retainer of the earl who had been sent south to gather news of the battle, entered the orchard and approached the earl.

Northumberland advanced to meet him and asked eagerly, 'Now Travers, what good tidings bring you?'

'Alas, my Lord,' Travers answered, 'I have it on excellent authority that all is lost. Brave Hotspur lies dead, an arrow deeply embedded in his brain. King Henry and Prince Hal have won the day.'

'My son, what have they done with the body of my son? I know these scions of the House of Lancaster too well.'

'It pains me to say it.'

'Speak, man.'

'His body was salted and set up in the marketplace. Later it will be quartered and sent to the four corners of the country for public display. The head, Henry has decreed, will be impaled on the north gate of York.'

Elizabeth stared contemptuously at Northumberland and hissed, 'If you had done your duty instead of cowering under the bed sheets, my Hotspur would be alive today.'

Lady Northumberland said softly, 'Elizabeth, he was your husband but he was my son.'

Elizabeth answered, 'Who will call me Kate, now he has gone?'

Ignoring the women, Northumberland continued to question Travers. 'What of Worcester and Douglas?'

'Prisoners both, Douglas to be held for ransom – Worcester to be tried for treason and certain to be executed.'

'I can expect no mercy from that pair.'

Travers, with the merest hint of contempt, answered, 'Not of necessity, my Lord. You were not at Shrewsbury and so did not take part in the rebellion. They will be fully cognisant of that. I'm sure.'

★

Rhisiart was becoming disillusioned with Owain Glyn Dŵr. He acknowledged that Owain's ruthless destruction of his relationship with Catherine and the appointment of Griffith Young as chancellor contributed to this disenchantment. Rhisiart had been disturbed when Owain had not joined Hotspur at Shrewsbury and, when he recalled Owain's refusal to go to Richard's aid at Flint, he began to have serious doubts about Owain's resolution. A firm friendship had developed between Rhisiart and Walter Brut, therefore he decided to seek out Walter and discuss these misgivings. Approaching Walter's small, austere room, he heard voices and on entering he found his friend engaged in an animated conversation with Griffith Young. The sight of the man who had usurped the chancellorship, a post that Rhisiart thought would be his, now appeared to be in the process of appropriating his only friend. Rhisiart banished such an ignoble thought and smiled amiably at Young.

It soon became apparent that Young had no intention of leaving, so this left Rhisiart the option of concealing his feelings or disclosing them to both men. He chose the latter, and, when he had finished his exposition of what he thought was Glyn Dŵr's lack of resolve, Young and Walter exchanged a meaningful look.

Young was the first to speak, 'Concerning Glyn Dŵr's failure to go to the aid of Richard at Flint, he was simply exercising the caution a wise commander should. He would have been marching to support a king who was bereft of power and the result would have been the destruction of his forces and the extinction of a Welsh rebellion before it had even started.'

Walter intervened, 'In the case of Owain's absence at the battle of Shrewsbury, he had previously warned Hotspur that, due to his commitments in Carmarthenshire, he would not be able to support him for at least a fortnight. And those commitments were by no means illusory. Early that July, Owain had led a general uprising in the Towy valley and was proclaimed Prince of Wales and oaths of fealty were sworn to him. He then led a force of 8,000 men to the west, creating panic among the English barons. The castles of Dryslwyn and Newcastle Emlyn fell to him and he laid siege to the town and castle of Carmarthen, both of which surrendered after two days.'

Rhisiart broke in, impatiently, 'But had he been with Hotspur at Shrewsbury, they would have won a victory that could have destroyed the House of Lancaster. A result far more significant than any he won in west Wales.'

Young smiled and said, 'Glyn Dŵr was thinking long term. His alliance with the Mortimers and Percys was likely to be an unstable one. Edmund Mortimer and Hotspur would have always taken an English view leaving Glyn Dŵr isolated. With the Percys destroyed, the odds were reduced to evens.'

This homily on the duplicity of great statesmen silenced Rhisiart.

'I was given an insight into Owain's character, during that campaign in west Wales,' Walter said. 'We were in Carmarthen and at a critical point in the operation, Owain had heard that the famous bard Hopcyn ap Tomos lived within riding distance. Hopcyn forecast the future through the medium of cywyddau brud, poems composed in an ancient language only intelligible to the elect of bards. Owain told me it was imperative that he consult Hopcyn and he wished me to escort him to Ynys Dawe on the banks of the Tawy where the bard lived. I protested that he would be passing through hostile territory and would need more than one escort. Owain retorted that he wished this visit to be secret. I then said that I could arrange for Hopcyn to be brought to him. But he would have none of it. You did not summon a prophet as if he were a groom.

'Disguised as two monks, we rode from the castle in the early hours of a bright summer's day. The countryside was at its best, the hedgerows garlanded with a multitude of flowers of diverse colours and, when we reached the coastal path, the golden rays of the sun bounced off the placid surface of the gently breathing sea. When we reached Hopcyn's spruce, white painted cottage, Owain knocked discreetly on the door, almost instantaneously the door opened and we were confronted with a large clean-shaven man, dressed in a costume which, in its discreet elegance, would not have looked out of place at King Henry's court. Anyone looking less like a conventional bard, it would be hard to imagine. On seeing Owain, he smiled and said that he had been expecting this visit, then, with a wave of the hand, he ushered us into the one room that constituted the entire interior of the cottage. The furnishings were simple but well made. Hopcyn and Owain sat facing each other at the table while I stood uncomprehending in a corner listening, as they spoke in that language known only to the bards and wizards of Wales. At one stage Hopcyn raised his voice as if issuing a warning and in response Owain's face flushed angrily. When we departed, the relationship between Hopcyn and Owain was far less cordial than when they met. On the journey back to Carmarthen, Owain told me that Hopcyn, on being asked by Owain to foretell the nature of his fate, told him in no uncertain terms that his fate was speedy capture under the black banner at a location on Gower.'

Rhisiart cried excitedly, 'So that was the reason why he curtailed the campaign. That is what stopped him leading the army into Gower, not the news of Hotspur's defeat.'

Walter said, 'I'm sure that defeat played some part in the decision, but the main thing that influenced him was Hopcyn's prophecy. Which shows that Owain's reputation as a sorcerer is based on more than his success in manipulating the elements to the disadvantage of his enemies. He was prepared to seek advice from other practitioners of the black art.'

'Of course,' Young said, 'the prophecy was in itself a deterrent.'

★

Despite Hotspur's defeat at Shrewsbury, Owain's earlier victory at Bryn Glas continued to attract increasing numbers of armed peasants to his cause. He now had several armies besieging English-held castles throughout Wales. There was one castle however that resolutely refused to yield, Carreg Cennen. Built on the summit of a steep hill four miles from Llandeilo, the castle presented to Owain and his 800 besiegers a dismaying impression of invincibility and defiance. The first feature that confronted Owain was an unusual outer defensive system that consisted of a series of bridges laid across deep pits. As Owain's men traversed these bridges, they were subjected to withering fire from archers placed in the formidable twin-towered gatehouse. When the defenders withdrew the bridges, they created a deep impassable chasm into which the hapless attackers were plunged. Owain, not willing to sacrifice more of his men, reluctantly abandoned the siege.

He enquired of Rhys Ddu, 'Who is the custodian of this fortress?'

Rhys Ddu replied. 'John Scudamore, a scion of the Scudamore family of Herefordshire. Not a family of great distinction, one of the lesser dynasties one might say.'

'Be that as it may, the young man has deployed the defences of the castle in an exemplary way. If our paths cross sometime in the future, I will shake his hand and tell him so.'

In August Owain attacked and captured the town of Cardiff and its castle. Aberystwyth and Harlech suffered the same fate. Owain, impressed with the strength of the castle at Harlech, moved in and made it his headquarters. Stung by these reverses, King Henry assembled a large army at Shrewsbury, and in early September set forth on what turned out to be a frustrating winter campaign. Owain, always cautious about deploying his men in a pitched battle, relied on the method of entanglement, of retreat and the use of natural obstacles and the weather. This resulted in Henry fruitlessly chasing Owain all over Wales. One evening Henry pitched his tent in a secluded valley only for a thunderous cloudburst during the night to bring his tent crashing down upon him. The fact that he was wearing his armour saved his life. Enemies and supporters alike attributed this natural occurrence to Owain's occult powers. Henry, acknowledging defeat, withdrew his forces to England, where he licked his wounds like a badly mauled lion.

The success he had attained and the accumulation of favourable auguries now led Owain to believe that he did possess supernatural powers and that he had been chosen to fulfil his people's desire for a free Wales. He felt as if he carried in his hands a precious glass vessel and was traversing a polished, slippery slope. He made a resolution. Nothing must interfere with his task. No sacrifice would be too great. He had already sacrificed the happiness of his daughter and Rhisiart in order to form an alliance with the Mortimers, and he must now cast out all those strange images of Alice leading his army to victory. From this time on, imperfect though he was, he would strive to be a man worthy of his mission.

CHAPTER 8
Poor mad King Charles

HARLECH CASTLE SEEMED to have grown naturally from the rock on which it stood. It was a perfect example of a concentric castle, where one line of defence is enclosed within another. The thick stone walls and tall round towers gave one an awesome impression of massive proportions and enormous strength. Its position on top of a vertical cliff facing the sea meant it was only vulnerable to attack from the east side. Accordingly the defences on that side were further strengthened. The upper floors of the gatehouse provided the main accommodation, while the lavishly furnished rooms on the top floor were for visiting dignitaries.

In his address to the first council of war he had held in Harlech castle, Glyn Dŵr was unable to suppress a note of triumphalism. When the loud applause died down, Chancellor Young rose to his feet and sounded a contrapuntal note of caution.

'Prince,' he said, 'while it is understandable to revel in our recent successes, I would point out that it was not purely through our own efforts that we are now in this happy situation. May I remind you that during Henry Don's attack on Kidwelly he was supported by men from France and Brittany. It was a flotilla of French ships, under the command of Jean d'Espagne that attacked the town and castle of Caernarvon. At Lleyn, six French ships landed with supplies for our army. Throughout this campaign, French ships aided us as we laid siege to the towns and castles of the coast. They have done this although no formal agreement has been signed between you and Charles VI. I propose that such an alliance be made without delay.'

It was agreed that Owain's brother-in-law, John Hanmer, and his chancellor, Griffith Young, would travel to France and seek an audience with Charles VI. There, as fully empowered commissioners, they would negotiate a treaty between Charles and Owain.

On the journey across the Channel, Young, who was well acquainted with the vagaries of European monarchies, informed Hanmer of Charles' volatile past.

Young said with a smile, 'Known as Charles the Well-loved when he was born, became Charles the Mad.'

'What caused such a cruel reversal?' Hanmer asked.

'From his mid-twenties on he has experienced bouts of psychosis, which recur to the present day. Once, when leading a cavalry charge, he turned his horse and attacked his own men, killing three of them before he was overpowered. Another time he refused to bathe and change his clothes for five months. There were periods when he did not recognise his own wife and child and ran wildly through the corridors of his Paris residence.'

'Poor man,' said Hanmer, shaking his head sadly. 'And this is the man Glyn Dŵr wishes us to negotiate with?'

'Oh, don't worry. I am reliably informed that he is at this time in one of his lucid periods.'

'Thank God for that. Let's hope it lasts.'

On arriving at the Hôtel Saint-Pol, Charles' Paris residence, they were met by Pierre Salmon, his secretary, who informed them that the King was in good spirits and anxious to meet them.

Charles was in animated conversation with his friend and confidant Olivier de Clisson when Salmon ushered Owain's two envoys into the room and introduced them to the French

King, who, with an elegant gesture of the hand, graciously bade them be seated. Hanmer looked anxiously at the King and thought he could detect an unnatural ferment behind those light blue eyes.

'Welcome to France, chevaliers,' Charles said excitedly. 'Please make the acquaintance of my very dear companion Olivier de Clisson. Did you know that I nearly lost him? He was the victim of a failed assassination plot. My reign has been a troubled one, but my good friends Pierre and Olivier have sustained me through the bad times.'

Here he smiled affectionately at the two Frenchmen and continued, 'Were I to strip to the waist you would see the scar tissue that resulted from serious burns I sustained in January 1392. The date is burned into my memory – the twenty-ninth of the month. At a royal celebration, I and four lords took part in a masque. We were dressed up as wild men and danced chained together. The costumes were made of linen cloth sewn onto our bodies and soaked in resinous wax, so we appeared hairy from head to foot. During the performance my brother Louis approached too near a man bearing a lighted torch and set us on fire. Have you ever experienced the smell of human flesh burning and then realised it was your own? I was the only one to survive, chained to four blackened corpses. I still do not know if it was an accident or an attempt at regicide.'

Young felt the moment had come to state the purpose of their visit, and in impeccable French he said, 'Your Majesty, we in Wales are well aware that you have never accepted the change of dynasty in England.'

His voice tight with anger, Charles replied, 'Accept the overthrow and murder of the sainted Richard? Never! Although France is not at war with England, I will take every opportunity to injure the government of that usurper Henry.'

Young made a sign to Hanmer, who fumbled in his cloak

and drew out a large sealed envelope, which he handed to Young.

Young then went down on his knees and offered the missive to Charles, with the words, 'Your Majesty, I have the honour to present you with a petition from the true Prince of Wales, Prince Owain Glyn Dŵr.'

Charles quickly passed the letter to Pierre Salmon and said pleasantly, 'I never read state documents myself, I leave that to my advisors. So if you would be kind enough to narrate a concise summary of the contents, I would be grateful.'

Young, having written the final draft, smiled confidently and said, 'My master, the high and puissant Prince Owain Glyn Dŵr states that he bows his knee to the mighty King of France with devotion and respect. He desires that they form an alliance that would bind the King and the Prince in close league against Henry of Lancaster.'

★

A month later, Young and Hanmer, after negotiations with the King's advisors, returned to Wales bearing a treaty that detailed the support Charles was prepared to give to the Welsh in their struggle against Henry. Although no specific commitment was made concerning a future invasion by French troops, the whole tenure of the agreement implied that such an event was very probable. This treaty was not the only thing they brought back from France. At their last meeting with Charles, he informed them that Glyn Dŵr's reputation as a great warrior had so impressed him he wished to send the prince a suitable gift. He then clapped his hands and three young pages entered bearing, on velvet cushions a gold helmet, a cuirass and a sword.

The first action Owain took on the return of his envoys

was to don the helmet and cuirass and make bold and sweeping gestures with the sword.

Rhisiart whispered to Young, 'If there is one thing Owain cherishes above all else, it's his reputation as a great warrior.'

Owain then sent Charles full information concerning the ports of Wales, thus making clear that he was expecting the arrival of a strong French expeditionary force in the not-too-distant future. Having established this strong alliance with the French, Owain now looked to renew the tripartite treaty with the Mortimers and Percys. His position was formidable and, from the top of the highest tower of the redoubtable Harlech castle, he looked with confidence to the future.

★

After Hotspur's defeat and death at Shrewsbury, the Earl of Northumberland spent a desperate few months waiting for the King to march on Warkworth castle and arrest him for high treason. Henry, however, contemptuously turned his back on the trembling earl, considering him to be a spent force. Once Northumberland realised that his neck was not at risk, his mind turned to thoughts of revenge. Therefore, when he received an invitation to attend a secret meeting with Glyn Dŵr and Edmund Mortimer at the archdeacon's house in Bangor, he accepted with alacrity. The man who was largely responsible for arranging this conference was Northumberland's ally Lord Bardolf, a former councillor of King Henry, and a man of eminence who, disaffected with Henry, had joined the rebels. He was a young man of thirty-five, with a rotund figure and a large bushy black beard. Despite his previous exalted status, he always deferred to Northumberland who was some thirty years his senior.

The meeting took place in early February and, though no one spoke of Hotspur, his absence hung over the gathering like Caesar's ghost at Philippi. Owain arrived with a mission, he was determined to fulfil prophecies made of the recovery by the Welsh of their ancient lands. He had set himself a formidable task, as those archaic boundaries enclosed large parts of England.

The first step was taken when the three magnates agreed that, after Henry's overthrow, the kingdom would be divided into three parts. It was at this point that Owain made his proposal for the boundaries of the new Wales.

Speaking resolutely, he said, 'The boundary of the Welsh nation will run along the Severn to the north gate of the city of Worcester, thence to the group of ash trees on the high road from Bridgnorth to Kinver, thence by the old road running north to the source of the Trent, thence to the source of the Mersey and along that river to the sea.'

Northumberland and Edmund stared in disbelief at Owain. The first to speak was Northumberland.

'God man!' he spluttered, 'You have incorporated a considerable part of England into this new Wales of yours.'

Owain countered fiercely, 'The part you refer to was Welsh in ancient times. The group of ash trees are known in Welsh fable as "Ouennau Meigion". Furthermore, over the years Welshmen, in increasing numbers, have been settling in those border areas.'

Edmund now intervened, 'Do you not think that by making such an extravagant claim, you are jeopardising this whole alliance?'

Owain turned in fury on Edmund, 'Of the three in this room, you are one with the least influence. Also you are my son-in-law, so all I expect from you is respectful silence. Extravagant claim indeed! The main assembly points for armies attacking Wales are Worcester, Shrewsbury and Hereford. That is why I want them under Welsh control.'

Owain paused before saying quietly, 'I have the backing of the French and if I withdraw from this enterprise, you lose the French.'

A frustrated Northumberland and a cowed Edmund gave way and agreed to Owain's demands. After further discussions, it was decided that Northumberland was to get the north of England together with much of middle England. Edmund was to receive southern England and his nephew was to be made king. The archdeacon, who had been present throughout the meeting, was given the task of writing a document incorporating the agreement, which was to be known under the grand title of The Tripartite Indenture.

*

It was late April 1404, Owain and his chancellor Griffith Young paced the battlements of Bronwen Tower. Both men were oblivious to the beauty of the shimmering sea as it lapped gently against the rock on which Harlech castle was founded. They were preoccupied with affairs of state.

'I have heard,' Young ventured, 'that John Trevor, Bishop of Bangor, has come over to our side.'

'Then he must be convinced that my ultimate success is no longer problematic and, as a fellow Welshman, wishes to do me homage.'

Young snorted and said, 'He has always been an ardent supporter of King Henry. This abrupt change of allegiance has more to do with the prelate ensuring his continued well-being than any desire to honour you.'

'O come, Chancellor, have more charity. The man is a doctor of law, as are you, and has an impeccable curriculum vitae. Consecrated in Rome, he attached himself to the cause of King Henry and served him loyally in parliament and the royal councils. As a Welshman he has spoken in parliament, urging that justice be done to the claims of the Welsh people.'

'Yes but only to prevent them rising in revolt. He was not really concerned with relieving their suffering.'

'How can you presume to understand the motives of others? Our bard Iolo Goch has praised, in two cywyddau, John Trevor's generosity and friendliness.'

'Yes, drooling on about the abundance of food and drink at the bishop's table. We all know that the quickest way to a bard's heart is through his stomach. Then what about that great gold ring with its shining ruby? Iolo says it is a talisman to shield the bishop from evil. It is more likely to be a symbol of his ostentation.'

Owain laughed and said, 'Anyone would think that you are afraid he will take your place at my side. I am sure that John Trevor has a genuine love of Wales and will serve me faithfully. But let me assure you Gruffydd Young, that he will never replace you in my heart.'

Young, looking embarrassed, murmured, 'There was no need for you to make that affirmation.'

'Now would seem to be the time to strike a decisive blow,' Owain said. 'My influence extends across Wales while Henry only has control of a pitiful number of castles and boroughs.'

Young responded eagerly, 'Yes, but first you must fulfil your promise made at Glyndyfrdwy to establish a national parliament for Wales. That would be the ideal time and occasion to have you formally crowned as Prince of Wales.'

'Yes, but where? It must be somewhere central and in an area controlled by me.'

'Machynlleth,' Young said without hesitation. 'It is a prosperous town and has a large barn-like townhouse that could house the parliament.'

CHAPTER 9
The first Welsh parliament

O WAIN PACED ANXIOUSLY about his chamber, his mind pulsating with fevered thoughts. His brain felt like some antic creature beyond his control. Now, on the eve of the first Welsh parliament, he was engulfed by a tidal wave of doubts and intimations of disaster. He felt a desperate desire for human contact. By the light of the feebly burning wall torches he saw Madoc asleep in a dark corner, his arms wrapped firmly about his axe. Owain bent low over the recumbent body and shook him by the shoulder. The bodyguard leapt to his feet, his axe raised in readiness to defend his prince.

Owain said sharply to the startled Madoc, 'Lay aside your axe, there is no danger but I'll not sleep tonight, my spirit is too troubled.'

'What troubles you, Sire?'

'I am but a man such as you are. All my senses and frailties are human. What has a king above an ordinary man, but ceremony? Take away ceremony and I am but a man. What troubles me are the lives I've sacrificed for my cause.'

'Your cause is a good one and so the sacrifices are acceptable.'

'But what if my cause is not good? I carry the guilt for all the legs, arms and heads chopped off in battle, and will suffer in hell for my sins.'

Over the many months that Madoc had stood guard over Owain – in the frenzy of battle and the danger-fraught hours of the dark night – Owain had become acutely aware of the steadfast loyalty with which Madoc had carried out his duties.

The relationship between the erudite prince and the simple soldier had grown into one of affection and trust.

'Master,' Madoc said, 'How can I, a peasant, talk meaningfully with you, a wise and scholarly prince?'

'We have often spoken together before. Believe me, I need your companionship tonight. You say I'm wise and scholarly, there must be some question you would like answered. Ask me.'

Madoc frowned with concentration and then asked, 'Does the white dragon stand for the English as the red dragon does for the Welsh?'

'Yes, my boy, you have it.'

'Well, where do these allusions come from?'

'Far back in history, myth and legend.'

'When?'

Owain had recovered his nerve. He had always harboured a desire to be a bard and believed that he could tell and embellish a tale as well as any poet. Now he was given the chance to prove it.

Settling himself in a chair and gesturing that Madoc do the same, he began, 'I'll start in the year 55 BC. You know what that means?'

'Of course I do,' Madoc said. 'Fifty-five years before the birth of Jesus.'

Owain nodded and then continued, 'At that time Britain was a land of grassy uplands, wild mountain ranges, marshy valleys and dense forests. The island was populated by Britons, an intelligent and warlike people who were divided into tribes. Each tribe had a chief or petty king. Foremost among these chiefs was Cassivellaunus who was regarded by the other chiefs as the King of all Britain. The Britons lived in simple round huts clustered together in small villages or surrounded by the walls of hilltop fortresses.

'In the year 55 BC the Roman legions, led by Julius Caesar, crossed from Gaul and invaded the southern coast of Britain. King Cassivellaunus rallied the British tribes and drove the Romans back to their ships. A year later Caesar returned. This time, the better armed and more disciplined Roman soldiers proved too strong for the Britons and King Cassivellaunus was forced to sue for peace. However, before Caesar could complete his conquest he had to return to Gaul to quell a revolt and so Britain escaped Roman domination for another hundred years. Then, in the year AD 43...'

'Forty-three years after the birth of Christ,' interjected Madoc.

Owain nodded and continued, 'The Emperor Claudius decided to bring Britain to heel once and for all. The King of the Britons at this time was Caractacus and for eight years he fought heroically against the Romans until he was betrayed and taken as a captive to Rome where he was dragged in chains through the streets behind the chariots of the triumphant Romans.

'His dauntless bearing so impressed Claudius that, with the words, "Rome knows how to pardon a brave enemy," he ordered that Caractacus be freed.

'In the years that followed, the Romans conquered the whole of southern Britain but were unable to subdue the Picts and Scots who dwelt in the northern part of the island. To stop these fierce tribesmen from attacking the part of Britain under Roman occupation, Emperor Hadrian built a great wall fortified along its entire length by forts manned by Roman soldiers. The Britons now enjoyed a long period of peace and prosperity.

'Roman engineers built us fine new towns linked by magnificent stone paved roads and Roman soldiers protected us from all invaders.

'This happy state of affairs lasted until the year AD 410 when all the Roman legions were recalled to protect Rome from the Barbarians, and the Britons were left to defend themselves against the Picts and Scots from the north and the Saxons from the sea. At this unhappy time the Britons chose Constantine to be their King. He married a lady of noble family and sired three sons Constans, Aurelius Ambrosius and Uther Pendragon. When ten years had passed, there came a certain Pict seeking a private conversation with Constantine. As soon as Constantine ordered his guards to leave them alone, the Pict drew out a dagger he had concealed in his cloak and stabbed Constantine to death.

'Constans was now given the kingship and he made Vortigern, who was a minor chieftain, his principal advisor. His trust in Vortigern, however, was sadly misplaced. Vortigern bribed the King's own guards and one night they burst into the chamber where Constans lay asleep and cut off his head, which they stuck on the end of a spear and carried to Vortigern. The wily Vortigern, pretending to be horrified, ordered the assassins to be executed on the spot and then proclaimed himself King. Ambrosius and Uther Pendragon, fearing for their lives, fled from the country with their followers. But they swore that one day they would return to avenge the murder of their brother.

'Now that he was King, Vortigern's troubles really started. Not only did he have the task of defending his kingdom from invaders eager to plunder its riches but he also lived in the constant fear that Ambrosius and Uther Pendragon would return seeking vengeance for their murdered brother Constans. One day there landed on the coast of Kent a large number of longships full of armed Saxon warriors under the command of two lords, Hengist and Horsa.

'Vortigern, in a desperate effort to gain allies, offered to allow these warriors to settle in Kent if they would help him against his enemies. The Saxons accepted his offer and for a number of years they supported Vortigern in many battles against the Picts and Scots. In one of these battles, Horsa was slain, but Hengist survived and as time went on he built up his strength by bringing more and more Saxons into Britain. When he felt powerful enough he rebelled against Vortigern. Many thousands of Britons were slain and Vortigern was forced to flee into the hills of Wales. When he reached Mount Erith, Vortigern's magicians advised him to build a great impregnable fortress on the top of the mountain so that he would be safe from Hengist's men, who were pillaging the country. Vortigern agreed and set his army to work immediately, but each time the foundation stones of the castle were laid they sank into the earth and vanished. The magicians tried one magic spell after another but to no avail. As Hengist and his men drew nearer and nearer, Vortigern paced around the walls of his non-existent castle and grew more and more frantic. He gave them one last chance to find a solution to the problem.'

At this point, Owain stopped speaking and sat very still with a slight smile playing around his lips.

'Oh do go on,' urged Madoc.

'Forgive me, Madoc, but I have now reached the point in the story where I really enter the realm of fantasy. This is where Merlin, makes his first appearance. Although he was at that time only a young boy living quietly with his mother in a small village in Wales, news of his magic powers had reached the ears of Vortigern's envious magicians. They told Vortigern that the only way to make the foundations of the castle firm was for Merlin to be killed and his blood sprinkled on the mortar and stones. You see, the solution they proposed, even if it did not make the foundations of the castle firm, would at least rid them of a dangerous rival.

'Vortigern ordered Merlin's arrest and he was brought before the King tied hand and foot ready for the sacrifice. Merlin was aware that he was standing on the top of a high mountain. The clouds scurrying overhead seemed so near he felt he could reach out his hand and unravel them from the sky. While far below, the countryside unrolled before his eyes – a patchwork of fields and woods. A tall warrior, whom Merlin realised was the King, as his helmet was surmounted with a circlet of gold, stepped forward and peered incredulously at the boy before him. He was flanked on either side by a number of old men, each with a long white beard and wearing the cloak of a magician.

'"You are Merlin the magician?" he asked, his voice clouded with suspicion. "I am," answered Merlin. His voice, though young, was without fear. "Why have I been brought here?"

'"So that you may be slain and your blood sprinkled on the foundations of my castle to make them firm."

'"Who advised you in this matter?" asked Merlin.

'"My magicians."

'"Then let them stand before me face to face so that I may question them and prove that they have lied."

'The King was amazed at Merlin's boldness and hesitated, not knowing whether to do as Merlin asked or kill him without further argument.

'The soldiers, impressed by Merlin's dauntless bearing, took up the cry, "Give him the chance. Let him confront the magicians."

'Vortigern summoned his wizards and they shuffled

reluctantly forward. Merlin gazed sternly at them and said, "You have recommended that my blood be sprinkled on the mortar and stones, because you are envious of me and wish my death."

"'Sire, this is not true," the magicians protested. "It is the only way to make the castle stand firm."

"'Tell me, then" ordered Merlin. "What lies hidden under the foundations that prevents the castle from standing firm?"

'The magicians stood dumb, unable to answer. "Answer," snapped Vortigern. "Answer," thundered the soldiers.

'But the wizards just stood there and said not a word, their faces seared with terror. "My Lord King," said Merlin. "These knaves can never answer for they do not know. Their ignorance is as great as their envy of me. Order your men to dig down deep in the earth and they will uncover a vast lake. That is what prevents you from building your castle."

'The soldiers were issued with tools and set to work. Merlin worked with a will, determined to play his part in proving that he was right. All day they dug and when night came, Merlin ordered that flaming torches be lit all around the area so that the work might continue throughout the night.

'With the dawn came success. Just when Merlin, worn out and covered in sweat and dirt, felt he could go on no longer, his spade splashed into water. Shouting encouragement to those around him he redoubled his efforts and in a short time there lay, glistening in the early morning sunshine, a beautiful expanse of blue water. Vortigern was called from his hut and hurried down to the edge of the lake, where he stood gazing in awe at the confirmation of Merlin's prophecy. Merlin turned in triumph to where the evil wizards cowered together. "Tell me wise ones," he mocked. "What lies beneath the waters of this lake?"

'A strange stillness descended as everyone waited for the magicians to answer, but yet again they remained dumb. With a shrug of contempt, Merlin turned his back on them and addressed Vortigern, "My Lord, if you drain this lake you will find at the bottom two caves. In these caves are two dragons – one red, the other white."

'"How is one to drain so vast a lake," asked Vortigern. "Surely, ten thousand men with ten thousand buckets could labour for ten thousand days and not empty it."

'Merlin laughed, "No no, Sire, forgive me but that would be a stupid way of doing it. We must dig a channel from the side of the lake to the edge of the cliff. The water will then flow along the channel and down the side of the mountain."

'After a breakfast of bread and wild honey the soldiers were once again swinging their spades. The lake was very near the edge of the cliff and it was not long before the ditch was completed. To prevent the water flowing into the channel and drowning them as they worked, a strong barrier of wood had been secured at one end of the channel. This was held in place by a rope and Merlin was chosen to cut the rope and release the water. He strode to the end of the lake. Grasping the hilt of a sword with both hands, he raised it high above his head and brought it crashing down to slice cleanly through the rope. The barrier fell. The water rushed into the channel and flowed over the cliff edge to form the greatest waterfall Merlin had ever seen.

'Looking down, Merlin saw two caves at the bottom of the pit left by the receding water. As if awakened by the noise of the rushing water, two dragons emerged slowly and menacingly from the caves – one a dark and angry red, the other a dazzling and pure white. The bank was now crowded with soldiers all staring in wonder at the two strange creatures. So great was the crush that a poor unfortunate lost his footing and fell screaming into the pit. The white dragon lazily turned its head towards the terrified soldier, opened its great jaws and emitted a searing tongue of flame. Before their horrified eyes the watchers on the bank saw the soldier burn up in an instant. All that was left of him was a smear of grey ash on the mud floor of the pit.

'The dragons now became aware of each other. The white dragon bore down on the red one and a terrible battle ensued. The air was filled with smoke and the sounds of tearing flesh as they snorted great clouds of fire and tore at each other with their fearsome claws. The red dragon appeared to weaken and, sensing the kill, the white dragon drove it back. But just when it seemed that the red dragon would be torn to pieces, its strength revived and it now drove the white dragon back. Despite this brave recovery, however, it soon became clear that the red dragon was doomed. The anguished sounds of battle ceased, the air cleared to reveal the inert form of the red dragon with the cruel talons of the white dragon pressing it into the mud. With a mighty bellow of triumph the white dragon returned to its lair.

'Vortigern and his men stood petrified, unable to fathom the meaning of what had occurred.

'Merlin's voice broke the silence. "Alas! The red dragon represents the people of Briton while the white dragon symbolises the Saxons, whom you invited into this land. I prophesize that the race that is now oppressed shall prevail in the end, for it will resist the savagery of the invaders. Build your castle Vortigern, for the foundations will now be solid and not sink into the ground."

'For many days and nights Vortigern's soldiers laboured at the task until a tall elegant castle stood proudly on the mountain top.

'Merlin addressed Vortigern for the last time. "Ambrosius and Uther Pendragon, together with their faithful British followers, are already on the high seas making for this land of Briton, determined to avenge the murder of their brother Constans. First they will defeat the Saxons then they will seek you out and kill you."

'Vortigern arrogantly answered, "I will seek safety in my impregnable castle and laugh in their faces." Merlin smiled and said softly, "A wise choice, Sire. I can assure you that no siege-weapon exists that can breach the walls of this castle." Reassured, Vortigern entered his castle to await the assault of his foes.'

Owain paused and then said, 'There we have one of the first references to the red and white dragons.'

'Don't stop there,' Madoc pleaded. 'What happened to Vortigern when his enemies caught up with him?'

'When Ambrosius and Uther Pendragon landed they quickly defeated the Saxons but Hengist escaped. The Britons then set out to find and kill Vortigern. Their army encircled his impregnable castle and launched a ferocious assault on its walls, to no avail. Vortigern stood on the top of its battlements and poured scorn on the besiegers.

'Ambrosius gazed up in despair and lamented, "The walls are too strong to be breached and too tall to be scaled." Uther Pendragon said, "Do not despair brother. His castle may be unassailable but we can burn him alive inside it."

'The Britons shot hundreds of burning arrows into the castle and set fire to its interior. They then stood back and watched with satisfaction as Vortigern burned to death.'

Owain chuckled and said, 'That was the one prophecy

Merlin did not tell Vortigern – that he would be burned to death in his own indestructible castle.'

'Some lad that Merlin,' said Madoc. 'Where did all this information come from?'

'The main source is a book written by Geoffrey of Monmouth in which he traced the history of the Britons through a period of nineteen hundred years.'

Madoc persisted, 'Yes, but where did he get his facts from?'

'Well, Geoffrey said that he was given an ancient book written in Welsh and he translated it into Latin. But, to my knowledge, no such book or manuscript has ever been found. Some scholars have been uncharitable enough to assert that Geoffrey made most of it up.'

'Well he writes a good story. Who became King after Vortigern?'

'That will have to wait until another night. This morning we ride to open the first Welsh Parliament.'

Word reached David Gam that Owain intended to hold a parliament at Machynlleth. Realising the increased credibility Owain would gain by such an action, Gam devised a plot to bring the proceedings to a bloody halt even before they started.

It was a bright sunny June morning when Owain, accompanied by his housecarls, set out for the townhouse in Machynlleth. The doubts that had tormented him the previous night were banished by a new-found resolution. At last he was about to lay the first foundation stone on which he would build an independent Wales and secure forever a significant place in the history of his nation.

That morning Gam also set out for that same townhouse, but his mind was seething with a hatred as warped as his mis-shapen body, hidden beneath his black cloak. This hatred was born from the circumstance that Gam's family had flourished under the rule of English monarchies and Owain's rebellion threatened that hegemony. It was made more virulent when Owain broke Hywel Sele's back and left him to die an agonising death in the hollow of an oak tree – Sele was Gam's lover.

Knowing that many of the delegates would be unknown to each other, Gam, together with his fellow assassins, mingled with the crowd gathered outside the parliament building, awaiting the arrival of Owain. There was a murmur of quiet excitement as Owain and his men arrived. The delegates parted, providing a path through to the entrance. As Owain crossed the threshold, Gam gave the signal and his men unsheathed their swords and attempted to hack their way through Owain's bodyguards and butcher the prince. Owain's men were well trained and fought back vigorously. Madoc, swinging his huge axe and spreading a bloodied circle of death and destruction, set the example that the others followed. Dancing with frustration and fury, Gam was forced to order his men to retreat, leaving their dead and wounded, and flee to their horses which they had tethered further up the road.

Maredudd urged his father to pursue the miscreants but Owain said firmly, 'No my son, we have more important business within.'

There in Machynlleth, in a ceremony reminiscent of the one that took place at Glyndyfrdwy on the morning of September 16th, in the year 1400, Owain Glyn Dŵr unambiguously proclaimed himself Prince of Wales and claimed the full trappings of royalty. The members of parliament were drawn from every region of Wales and were men of rank and substance. Also present were envoys from Scotland and France and, in a private meeting after the proceedings, the French renewed their promise of assistance in the war against Henry.

Just when Owain was congratulating himself on a goal achieved, a very angry John ap Thomas forced his way into Owain's presence.

'Why if it isn't our very own Wat Tyler,' Owain said jocularly. 'What ails you man? Why so choleric? Haven't I given you the parliament you craved?'

'Put not your trust in princes,' Thomas retorted. 'What mockery of a parliament is this? Every delegate a magnate – not a common man among them.'

Owain put an arm on Thomas' shoulder and drew him aside.

'I know this is not the parliament I promised, it was established merely as a suitable setting for my coronation. It had to be done swiftly while fortune was with me. This meant that there was no time to elect four men from each region. The next parliament will be properly established and the delegates will be truly representative of the people. This is what my rebellion is all about. Trust me, Thomas.'

CHAPTER 10

The rebellion falters

I N FRANCE, CHARLES was anxious to fulfil his promise to Glyn Dŵr and to this end he summoned the Count of La Marche who, with Jean d'Espagne, had provided invaluable support to Glyn Dŵr's attacks on the coastal towns of Wales the previous year. La Marche was well aware of his King's bouts of psychosis, so on arriving at the Hôtel Saint-Pol, he glanced uneasily at Pierre Salmon, who smiled encouragingly and gave him the thumbs-up sign. Charles was in an excitable state but was very explicit in what he wanted La Marche to achieve.

'I am putting you in command of a flotilla of sixty ships and giving you orders to carry five hundred armed cavaliers and two hundred crossbowmen safely over the Channel and land them on the Welsh coast. Understand?'

'Yes, Sire,' La Marche answered.

'Good. Go prepare the fleet and muster the men. Then report back here and I will give you more detailed instructions. Time is of the essence and Glyn Dŵr is depending on me.'

Within a month La Marche had prepared the fleet and mustered the men. But when he returned to the Hôtel Saint-Pol, he found his entrance to the royal apartments barred by Pierre Salmon and Olivier de Clisson.

'I'm afraid, my friend, you will not be having an audience with the King today,' said a grim faced Salmon.

'Why not?' La Marche asked.

'Because at this moment the King of France, stark naked and carrying an unsheathed sword, is chasing his terrified wife through the rooms and corridors of the royal apartments,' Clisson replied.

'One of his bouts of psychosis?' La Marche asked.

Salmon and Clisson both nodded gravely.

'But what am I to do?' La Marche demanded. 'I have sixty ships carrying seven hundred men-at-arms, together with their equipment and horses, ready to sail out of Breton and Norman harbours.'

'Don't panic,' Salmon said. 'Set sail and wait in the Channel until the King is capable of making a rational decision.'

Clisson added reassuringly, 'Once the guards have captured him and the physicians have sedated him, we'll get a decision out of him.'

Throughout the summer and autumn, La Marche sailed his flotilla up and down the Channel waiting for orders from Paris that never came. He never took his ships within sight of the Welsh coastline. Throughout this time Glyn Dŵr stood on the battlements of Harlech castle gazing out to sea hoping to see the approach of the French. While in Paris, Charles continued to chase his increasingly exhausted wife around the Hôtel Saint-Pol.

★

The non-appearance of the French was a considerable frustration for Owain, who felt the momentum of his rebellion was being dissipated by these months of inaction. In March 1405 he called a council of war with the intention of outlining his plans for further military action, without the support of the French. Before the meeting, wishing to receive his wife's approval of the plans he was about to place before the council, he visited his wife in her quarters. The previous night had been unseasonably close and disrupted by frequent thunderstorms. It soon became obvious to Owain that the Arglwyddes had had a disturbed night.

'My dear,' he said gently, 'I have decided that the time has come for me to lead a major assault upon the English.'

Her reaction was one of fearful incredulity.

'What do you mean, Owain?' she cried. 'Attack the English by all means, we have remained idle for too long waiting for that madman Charles to act, but for you to lead the assault is out of the question.'

Owain reacted angrily, 'Of course I must lead the assault. It is the inviolate duty of a prince to stand in the first rank, not skulk in the rear.'

'This past night as I dreamt, I saw a statue of you, Owain Glyn Dŵr, that, like a fountain, ran pure blood and your smiling subjects bathed their hands in it.'

'Cowards die a thousand deaths, the valiant die but once. You have misconstrued the dream entirely. My statue spouting blood in which my people bathed their hands signified that from me Wales will suck reviving blood.'

The Arglwyddes went down on her knees before him.

'Owain, Prince of Wales and my husband, listen to my words. I have consulted the auguries and the sights they have revealed frightened me as I have never been frightened before.'

Owain appeared shaken by her words and left the room without saying a word.

Standing in the great hall of Harlech castle, Owain addressed his advisors and lieutenants, 'My power now extends throughout Wales and in the mountainous regions no one dares challenge my authority. But will this situation survive in the future? Will it, without French support, survive determined English assaults? Well, I tell you this, it will not if we stay inactive, resting on our laurels. We must take the battle to the English before they launch a devastating attack that will exploit our weaknesses and bring crashing down about our heads the concept of an independent Wales. Attack is the best form of defence.'

Rhys Gethin rose to his feet in great excitement and proclaimed, 'At last after all these months of waiting for the laggard French to show their faces, we are going to get up off our knees and strike a blow at the old enemy. We must choose a target that the English consider important and will defend with a considerable force, thus the impact of our victory will be enhanced and momentum restored to our rebellion.'

'Grosmont!' Rhisiart exclaimed. 'Grosmont is a large and important settlement.'

'Only Abergavenny and Carmarthen are larger in the whole of south Wales,' Brut remarked.

Owain, sensing it was time to take control of the proceedings again, turned to his captain and said, 'Rhys Gethin, You will take 8,000 men and raze Grosmont and its castle to the ground. If Prince Hal sends an army to prevent you, destroy it.'

'You of course, Prince, will be at our head,' Rhys exclaimed.

For an instant, Owain hesitated then said firmly, 'No, I must stay here and prepare for the next parliament, which I intend to hold here in Harlech castle. A parliament in which I will establish the constitution of an independent Wales. Furthermore, I have consulted the oracles, and the omens for my safety in this coming affray are not good. There will be other opportunities in the future when I can lead you.'

Owain's decision not to take part in the attack on Grosmont dismayed his lieutenants and closest advisors, who, nevertheless, remained loyal and firmly believed in his integrity. For Rhisiart, however, Owain's decision revived his doubts about his master's resolution.

When speaking to Brut, he said bitterly, 'I believe that Owain regards us as merely the spokes in the wheel of his ambition.'

Brut replied, 'Those are unworthy thoughts. I believe in the man and his mission. I've asked him to allow me to accompany Rhys Gethin in the attack on Grosmont.'

Rhisiart said despondently, 'Since Young became his chancellor, my influence here has become negligible, and so I may as well join you.'

When Rhys Gethin and his force of 8,000 men reached Grosmont, they found the town virtually undefended, and lost little time in burning it to the ground. Walter Brut and Rhisiart had no heart for such wanton devastation as they stood against a background of fiercely ascending flames and beneath a sky polluted with obnoxious black clouds.

'We should have attacked the castle, which has a garrison to defend it, rather than this unwarranted onslaught against defenceless citizens. At least there would have been honour in that,' Rhisiart said bitterly.

Brut gave a laugh and said, 'Believe me Rhisiart, the opportunity for our brave captain, Rhys Gethin, to enhance his honour will come when Prince Hal receives news of our exploits.'

★

Fully recovered from the injury he sustained at Shrewsbury, Prince Hal was stationed at Hereford. On being informed of the carnage at Grosmont, Hal summoned John Talbot, the son of Richard, the fourth Baron Talbot, to his presence. John was a young man who had already established a formidable reputation as a military commander. The two young men, who embodied the flower of English chivalry, embraced.

Hal's orders were firm and concise, 'Take 10,000 men and avenge Grosmont.'

Gethin had finished the demolition of the town and was about to turn his attention on the castle when Talbot's force fell upon the Welsh from the rear. The battle soon degenerated into a mêlée of individual combats into which Brut and Rhisiart threw themselves with abandon, despite their previous misgivings. Gethin fought like a lion and destroyed all who came up against him until he was confronted by John Talbot, arrayed in a magnificent suit of armour. Gethin was a formidable fighter with sword and lance but he was no match for an aristocrat who had learnt his skills in the tournaments of the English court. After a short but furious contest, Gethin lay dying from a sword thrust through his throat.

Talbot bent down and whispered in Gethin's ear, 'So die all thieving Welshmen who dare rise against the true anointed King.'

When news of the captain's death spread among his men, they fled, leaving their dead and dying to grace the field of battle.

John Talbot returned in triumph to Hereford where he informed Hal of the extent of his victory – more than 800 Welsh slain, including the formidable Rhys Gethin. To celebrate the humiliation of Owain Glyn Dŵr, Talbot brought back on a hurdle the body of Owain's captain and hung it in chains in the market square for the citizens to gawp at and abuse.

Among the prisoners, Talbot picked out Rhisiart and John Hanmer, and presented them to Hal.

'Your Highness,' he said mockingly, 'allow me to present two jewels that adorn the court of the rebel Glyn Dŵr – his secretary Owain ap Rhisiart and his brother-in-law John Hanmer.'

Prince Hal looked in distain at the two dishevelled and bloodstained figures standing before him.

'Hanmer?' Hal queried. 'You went as an envoy to Charles of France. That was a journey that proved unnecessary.'

Rhisiart spoke up, 'The fruits of that visit have yet to develop but when they do Owain Glyn Dŵr will reign in London.'

Hal laughed and said, 'Well I'd better send you and your friend to London in advance so that you can prepare a place for your prince.'

He turned to Talbot and said dismissively, 'Clap them in irons and escort them to the Tower of London.'

As Rhisiart and Hanmer were marched away, they both wondered whether Walter Brut had managed to avoid capture or was numbered among the dead.

At the height of the battle Brut had suffered a deep sword thrust in his right side, followed by a blow to the head that knocked him unconscious. When he came to his senses the battle was over and he was lying under a mound of corpses. Despite his wounds and under the cover of darkness, he painfully crawled from the field. One thing dominated his thoughts – he must, with the greatest possible speed, inform his prince of this crushing defeat. Obviously, crawling there on all fours was out of the question but, as a result of the slaughter, there were numerous riderless horses now peacefully champing the grass. Fighting the pain and his own weakness he managed to pull himself up into the saddle of a magnificent black stallion. Sitting straight backed, Walter Brut rode through the night to bring the news to Harlech.

★

Harlech castle lay enveloped in an insidious gloom, the outer manifestation of the apprehension that gripped all, from Owain to the lowest kitchen drudge. They carried out their duties like automatons, their thoughts with Rhys Gethin and his army on the battlefield around Grosmont castle. The outcome was vital to the Welsh. They had suffered a number of reverses in the past months, and there was still no sign of a French invasion. Owain had established two centres of command, one at Harlech, for military operations, the other at Aberystwyth, where Owain's chancellor, Dr Young, controlled the affairs of the church in Wales. Dr Young, increasingly concerned with the military situation, had travelled from Aberystwyth seeking a meeting with Owain. It might strike one as slightly odd for a priest to meddle in military matters, but Dr Young thought he had an ecclesiastical solution to the problem.

It transpired that when Walter Brut, bloodied but unbowed, pulled up his horse outside the gates of Harlech castle, Owain and Young were closeted together in Owain's study. The first person to greet Brut when he staggered into the castle was Owain's eldest son. Gruffydd was his usual scowling, disgruntled self but, when he realised the extent of Brut's wounds, he swiftly summoned the medical staff and had the Lollard carried to a bed in one of the guest rooms. On being informed that Brut had returned from Grosmont, Owain and Young hurried to his bedside, anxious to obtain news of the battle. One look at the wounded man's face was enough to convince Owain that the Lollard was a dying man.

'Walter, how went the battle?' Owain asked gently.

A tear rolled down Walter's cheek and he answered, 'How I wish I could bring you news of a glorious victory but instead I am the bearer of dismal tidings.'

Gasps of despair came from a small group at the back of the room. Owain turned and saw the Arglwyddes, Catherine and Alice standing in the doorway. With a gesture of his hand he ordered them to be silent and turned his attention back to Walter.

'We had completed the destruction of the town,' Walter continued falteringly, 'and were about to attack the castle when we were overwhelmed by a force of 10,000 men under the command of John Talbot. Your captain fought like a lion but was eventually slain by Talbot, and once news of his death spread among our soldiers, they lost heart and fled the field.'

'Rhys Gethin slain?' asked Owain.

'Yes and hundreds more of our countrymen,' Walter answered.

Catherine now ran forward and grasping Walter's hand asked, 'Rhisiart what news of him? Does he lie among the dead?'

Walter hesitated and then said, 'I fought alongside Rhisiart and John Hanmer until I suffered a blow to the head and lost consciousness. When I recovered I could find no trace of them. They could be prisoners or they could be numbered among the dead.'

Owain now noticed a change in Walter's pallor that indicated the Lollard was on the cusp of death and he ordered everyone out of the room.

As Alice turned to leave, he touched her on the shoulder and said, 'Walter Brut is your husband and it is your duty to be at his side when he dies.'

Without a word, Alice took up her position at the side of her dying husband and gazed down at his poor wounded body. Her face evinced no emotion. When Owain laid his hand on her shoulder and stared into her defiant eyes, all those images of her as a heroic symbol returned to haunt him again.

News slowly filtered through that Rhisiart and Hanmer had been conveyed to the Tower where they now lay fettered in its dank dungeons. Owain did not appear too troubled by this but when he learnt that the corpse of Rhys Gethin was hanging in chains in the market square of Grosmont for the delectation of the citizens, his eyes filled with angry tears for the desecration of the body of his irascible old comrade in arms.

★

It was clear to Owain that, in order to restore credibility to the rebellion, they must strike back immediately.

Owain warned his lieutenants, 'To regain the initiative, it is imperative that our attack is crowned with success. Another defeat and we will start the long slide to oblivion.'

Gruffydd gave a harsh laugh and said, 'Then make sure our force is a large one and competently led.' Then as an afterthought he added, 'And the target a soft one.'

Owain, bristling with anger, shouted, 'Rhys Gethin was a courageous commander and a better man than you, my son.'

Madoc, standing guard at Owain's side as always, now intervened, 'As for who should lead us, there is only one answer. You, Owain, are our prince and you should be our commander on the battlefield.'

Before Owain could answer, the Arglwyddes said sharply, 'The parliament will be meeting here in May and it is unthinkable that our prince be not present.'

Gruffydd saw his opportunity and said, 'Of course, Father, you must preside over the first parliament to be held in Harlech. Therefore, I as your son will take your place at the head of the army. The only other contender, poor Maredudd, is lying wounded in his chamber. Your brother, Tudor, can come along as my deputy.'

Tudor smiled and quipped, 'We are so much alike, Owain, that the English will think I'm you.'

Owain joined in the laughter and said, 'That's the reason the English think I can be in two places at the same time. It adds to my reputation as a sorcerer.'

There followed a heated discussion on which castle they should attack and eventually the choice fell on Usk, after Gruffydd assured them that it was the least well defended. Before Gruffydd and his men set off, Henry Don who had been successfully defending Owain's interests in south Wales, arrived with a detachment of cavalry and insisted on joining the expedition. This made it more difficult for Owain to refuse Edmund Mortimer's strident demand to join in the action.

Summoning Edmund to his study, Owain spoke bluntly, 'Listen Edmund, you are more valuable to me as a symbol than you could ever be as a warrior. You get killed on the battlefield and I lose one leg of the tripartite alliance. Of what use is a two-legged stool? Look man, I too have become a symbol. Why do you think I was not with Rhys Gethin at Grosmont?'

Edmund tried to argue, but Owain raised his hand imperiously and command, 'Stop! Can you imagine how frantic Catherine would be if you went off to war? The last thing I want at this time is a hysterical daughter. Let this be the end of the matter.'

Gruffydd set off for Usk with his spirits high. 'Now at last,' he thought, 'I have the opportunity to show my father the true worth of Gruffydd ab Owain Glyn Dŵr. That wimp Maredudd, still licking wounds he suffered in some minor skirmish, is no worthy son of the warrior prince. Owain's other sons are nondescript, some not involved with the rebellion, others performing subordinate roles. Of Owain's sons, I am the only credible heir.'

He would not have been as sanguine had he known of the changes that had taken place in Usk. On the battlements of Usk castle stood a figure that in the dusk appeared to be that of a gorilla. Closer inspection however would reveal that it was David Gam, the fanatical admirer of all things English, who, back in the year 1401, had attempted to intercept Rhisiart's convoy as it escorted Owain's family to the sanctuary in Snowdonia. The intervening years had done nothing to ameliorate his hatred of Owain and the Welsh rebellion. Sensing the direction that Owain's attack would take, Gam had hurried to Usk and, using his local knowledge, he won over local Welshmen to turn against Owain and join the castle garrison. He also supervised the strengthening of the castle's defences. When Gruffydd stood in front of the gates of Usk castle, he had no idea of the strength of numbers that faced him inside the castle nor of the enhanced defences he would have to overcome.

★

In Harlech the parliament had come and gone. Looking back on the event, Owain took satisfaction from the fact that the participants were genuinely representative of the people of Wales – four good and honest citizens from every cymwd in Wales.

'That should please John ap Thomas,' Owain thought.

However, the assembly had only sat for three days before rumours of a large contingent of English troops approaching Harlech, sent the delegates scattering in all directions – the two envoys from France fleeing the fastest. The rumours proved to be false but the damage had been done. Owain was now fully aware of the importance of the battle Gruffydd was waging at Usk. Victory would restore his aura of invincibility and encourage the French to invade. Defeat would presage disaster. The Arglwyddes suddenly became concerned for the safety of her son Gruffydd and, in a complete reversal of her previous attitude, repeatedly urged Owain to go to his assistance at the siege of Usk castle. Edmund again pleaded that he be allowed to join Gruffydd, while his wife Catherine pleaded that Owain would keep him safe at Harlech.

Thoroughly exasperated, Owain cried out, 'Was ever a man so pestered in his own house by an importunate son-in-law and a pair of nagging women? This is my final word on the matter. Edmund remains here in Harlech. I remain in Harlech. We all remain in Harlech. Our fate now lies in the hands of Gruffydd and may God grant him victory.'

*

Arriving at Usk, Gruffydd was surprised to find the town and the surrounding area deserted. He immediately assumed that, hearing of his approach, the population had fled in terror. Henry Don, being a soldier who had fought in many campaigns, warned Gruffydd that there was a strong probability that, far from fleeing, the men had joined the garrison of the castle. Gruffydd dismissed this theory and, without preparing a plan of action that would cover all eventualities, impetuously launched an attack on the castle. Although Reginald Grey was the nominal commander of the garrison, it was David Gam who organised the defence. His apelike figure could be seen scurrying from one defensive point to another, directing operations. As the Welsh attempted to scale the battlements they were subjected to a continuous hail of arrows and their scaling ladders, heavy with soldiers, were pushed from the walls, sending the men screaming to their deaths below on the stony ground. Attempts to batter down the gates were repulsed with cauldrons of burning oil. Sickened by the slaughter, Henry Don and Tudor pleaded with Gruffydd to call off the siege and regroup but Gruffydd, incensed by the sight of David Gam leering down at him, insisted that the attack continued.

Suddenly the gates were thrown wide open and the garrison poured out in significant numbers. They sent the demoralised Welsh into headlong retreat. Henry Don, realising that a crushing defeat was now inevitable, sought to save his cavalry to fight another day. He ordered his horsemen to form a line three rows deep, then, with John ap Thomas at his side, he led his men forward at a brisk trot. Each man stood upright in his high-backed, padded saddle, a lance under his right arm, leaving his left free to manage the reins. As they approached the advancing enemy, Henry Don gave the order to charge and they broke into a full-blooded gallop. This charge faced none of the hazards that a cavalry experiences when charging an entrenched body of archers – the persistent hail of arrows and the hidden stakes driven into the ground and only revealed at the moment of impact. They charged clean through the enemy lines and were free. He found it hard to leave the infantry to their fate but he believed that this was the way to serve his prince. He would ride to Harlech and report to Owain and then return to his base in south Wales and continue to defend Owain's interests there.

Gruffydd and Tudor were caught up in the frenetic retreat that went through the river Usk and into the Forest of Monkswood, where, at the foot of the mountain Mynydd Pwll Melyn, 1,500 Welsh soldiers were slain. Among them was Tudor. When his body was discovered, his likeness to his brother Owain caused great excitement, but David Gam pulled off Tudor's helmet to reveal a shock of golden hair.

'Owain Glyn Dŵr's hair is grey,' he said dryly. 'This corpse is merely that of his brother.'

Owain's son Gruffydd survived the battle and was taken prisoner. Not content with the slaughter he had inflicted on the Welsh, David Gam, who was determined to heap more humiliation on Owain, chose at random 300 prisoners and lined them up in front of Usk castle. He then forced a manacled Gruffydd to watch as he had each one of them beheaded. The atrocity took over an hour to complete and at the end the executioners waded through blood.

Defiantly staring into David Gam's gloating face, Gruffydd snarled, 'Blood is the food of the devils in Hades. May you soon join them.'

Gam replied, 'Be grateful your head is not floating on that sea of blood below. May you rot in the Tower, together with your compatriots. I am told that London is again in the grip of the plague, so your sojourn there will be a short one.'

★

Henry Don reported to Owain that the Welsh attack on Usk had ended in abject failure and the loss of many lives. He then hurried off to his headquarters to prepare for the English invasion which he felt would follow David Gam's success. Over the following days the returning wounded brought horrifying details of the debacle, each new detail was a poisoned barb to Owain. Traumatised, he retreated to the sanctuary of his study with the faithful Madoc standing guard outside the door. For two days and two nights he sheltered there, wrestling with the despair that possessed his soul, until Chancellor Young persuaded Madoc to let him enter the chamber. There, slumped in a chair in front of the desk, Young discerned Owain – a figure of grief, all head and hands.

Without turning to face Young, Owain said, 'I have conjured up images of those who have died or been imprisoned in the darkest dungeons fighting for my cause – Hotspur, Rhys Gethin, Walter Brut, Rhisiart, Tudor, John Hanmer, 300 headless figures followed by an endless line of anonymous warriors. It is an awesome thing for a prince to send men into battle for a cause. Men will be slain and their deaths are laid at his door. If the cause be just he can bear the burden but what if the cause be unjust?'

Young answered gently, 'Fear not Sire, your cause is the right of a nation to live in freedom.'

'You know, Young, what I fear is that our troops are not equipped by nature and experience to win a pitched battle against the English. A swift attack and then run appears to be our only tactic.'

'We need more strategy and less gymnastics,' Young quipped and immediately regretted his flippancy.

Ignoring the remark, Owain continued, 'This defeat at Usk could well mark the end of my rebellion. Support is seeping from me, while Henry and his son Hal are assembling a massive force for an invasion that will sweep us from this land into the sea.'

CHAPTER 11

The French sail into Milford Haven

U NKNOWN TO OWAIN and his chancellor, a significant
meeting was taking place in Paris. Those in attendance
were the highest military figures in France and included
Jean de Hangest, Lord of Hughesville and master of the
crossbowmen; Jean de Roux, marshal of France; Renault de
Tire, admiral; Patrouillart de Trie and Robert de la Heuzé.

Hangest, who had diplomatic as well as military experience,
spoke first. 'I need not remind you of the abortive mission led
by Count La Marche last year.'

Robert de la Heuzé, who on account of his deformity was
known as Strabo, interrupted, his one eye blazing with anger,
'The man never set foot upon Welsh soil. My God, what an
infernal disgrace!'

Hangest continued, 'I agree, a disgraceful blot on the
escutcheon of a nation of proud warriors. It must never
happen again. This time we, the military, will organise the
expedition and see that it is carried through.'

His avowal was met with general acclaim and, true to his
word, an expeditionary force consisting of 800 men-at-arms,
600 crossbowmen and 1,200 light-armed troops set sail from
Brest and headed for Wales. The date was July 22nd, 1405,
and all those notables who had taken part in the Paris meeting
were aboard. It was a case of them putting their bodies where
their mouths had been.

★

News of the impeding arrival of a large French expeditionary force transformed the fatalistic gloom that reigned in Harlech castle to a mood of messianic euphoria, and brought supporters flocking back to Owain's banner. Such was the revival of Owain's fortune that, when Jean de Hangest anchored his armada in Milford Haven's spacious harbour, he was greeted by Owain Glyn Dŵr and 10,000 cheering Welshmen. A pale-faced Hangest informed Owain that the passage had been a stormy one and many of the horses had perished for lack of fresh water.

Not all of Owain's entourage were thrilled by the arrival of the French. Madoc eyed the elegantly armoured knights with scepticism, but laughed when, due to the loss of their magnificent stallions, they were forced to mount small sturdy Welsh ponies. It soon became apparent that the French had arrived with the intention of marching east towards the English border.

As Strabo so eloquently put it, 'My God, why do you think we have come here? I tell you, it is to march, shoulder to shoulder with our Welsh brothers in arms, across the border and subjugate England.'

Owain laid a reassuring arm on Strabo's shoulder and said, 'And so you shall my friend. But first I wish you to assist me in consolidating my position here in south-west Wales.'

Within a matter of days the allied forces captured the town of Haverfordwest but the castle was proving more obdurate. The bold Patrouillart de Trie, conspicuous in his shining black armour, rallied his men and led another desperate assault. This time, he succeeded in scaling the walls. There he fought like a tiger and scattered all before him until an arrow pierced his breastplate and he plunged from the ramparts. When he hit the ground the shank of the arrow broke off, leaving the head hidden under his armour. He was carried back to where Alice and other women of Owain's household were tending the wounded. Alice unhooked his breastplate and tore open his blood-soaked shirt to reveal the ugly wound.

'Pull out that accursed arrow head,' Patrouillart groaned.

Alice forced her fingers into his mutilated flesh and, firmly grasping the malignant lump of iron, tore it free. A fountain of bright blood shot skywards and drenched Alice in a scarlet flood.

The Frenchman gave a great shout, 'Pour le Royaume de France.' His head jerked back in the convulsion of death. Alice calmly turned her attention to the next wounded warrior.

Owain was so discouraged by Patrouillart's gruesome death that he abandoned the siege and moved on to Tenby, where an incident occurred that showed the two armies had not yet integrated into a single fighting unit. At the height of the siege, thirty English ships appeared over the horizon, and created such a panic that the French withdrew and were soon followed by Owain's men. When the English ships sailed past the harbour and out of sight, both armies shamefacedly returned to the fray. This so incensed Owain that, despite protests from the French leaders, he took on the role of overall commander and, within days, Carmarthen and Cardigan were in his hands. He was now able to acquiesce to the French demands that the army march east towards the border.

★

During the next few weeks, the combined army undertook a long victorious progress across south Wales, with Owain acting as an unofficial guide for his French guests. When they reached the Roman amphitheatre at Caerleon, Owain, to the considerable excitement of the French, explained that it was known as Arthur's Round Table. At the end of August, the army reached the border and invaded Herefordshire – Owain had crossed his Rubicon. Owain's reputation as a malign wizard, ensured that they met with little resistance, the villagers retreating and laying waste the land around them. This was of grave concern to Owain whose supply lines were being extended, while the English scorched earth policy was preventing him from living off the land.

When he shared this concern with Strabo who was riding beside him, the French knight stared fiercely at Owain with his one good eye and protested, 'Courage man! An army marches on its intent and not on its belly.'

'God,' Owain thought. 'How I hate this arrogant poltroon. How much better it would have been if he had perished at the siege of the castle at Haverfordwest instead of the noble Patrouillart de Trie.'

It was at that instant that they breasted a hill and were able to look down into the valley below. Owain could not believe the sight that confronted him. There nestling in a verdant valley stood a prosperous village bustling with citizens, blessed with barns bursting with grain and orchards heavy with fruit. Why they had not laid waste their village and fled – Owain was at a loss to understand. Maybe they were ignorant of his advance or they were sympathetic to his cause. Whatever the answer, he would be able to replenish his dwindling stocks. Owain's joy was short-lived as he saw a contingent of French skirmishers enter the village and proceed to burn every barn, slaughter the cattle, destroy every house and butcher every man women and child they could lay hands on. Owain, accompanied by his captains, rode furiously down the hill in an attempt to stop the mayhem, but by the time he arrived the hamlet was completely destroyed together with its inhabitants and livestock. The French knights remained at the top of the hill.

Strabo, looking a little puzzled, turned to his compatriots and said, 'What is the matter with the man? They were only peasants.'

This incident poisoned the relationship between Owain and his French allies. From that moment, Owain regarded them as elegant but also treacherous, insensitive brutes while they despised him as indecisive and lacking in the ruthlessness needed in a great leader. Despite this rupture in the relationship between the two allies, they continued their advance and reached Woodbury Hill two miles north of Worcester, where they set up a heavily fortified camp. Henry, who was at Leicester, now realised the serious nature of the situation he faced. If he did not act, middle England would be open to a full scale attack. Within three days he joined Prince Hal at Worcester and set up his camp on Abberley Hill. The two armies now faced each other on opposing hills. The scene was set for an epic showdown between the King and the rebel prince.

Standing on Woodbury Hill and gazing across at Henry's camp on Abberley Hill, Owain realised that he had reached a critical point in his campaign. The decision he would be called upon to make in the next few days would determine the success or failure of his rebellion. On the one hand he had the French leaders who eagerly urged him to attack Henry, take Worcester and march on to London. While his captains and his own cautious nature warned him that his supply lines were overstretched and that he was not in a position to sustain an advance deep into English territory. The two armies never engaged in battle. To the chagrin of the French, Owain ordered a withdrawal and led his troops in an orderly fashion back to the heart of Wales.

Henry and Hal watched in disbelief from Abberley Hill.

'Why did they not attack us?' Hal asked. 'They must

have known that, until our reinforcements arrived, they outnumbered us.'

Henry thoughtfully stroked the ends of his magnificent moustache before replying, 'Owain is a seasoned campaigner. Perhaps he thought that we would retreat into the city and he knows how thick the walls of Worcester are, and realised the paucity of his siege equipment.'

'But then he could have surrounded us and starved us into submission. Throughout, the Welsh have behaved as if we were laying siege to them.'

On arriving back in Wales, some of the French chose to stay with him, the rest returned to France in disgust.

Among those choosing to depart was, unsurprisingly, Strabo. In the final meeting between the two men the Frenchman vented his frustration on Owain, 'King Henry can sit at ease on his throne if you are his only protagonist. You lack faith in the ability of your own men to defeat the English and you lack the callousness needed to win.'

'You, Chevalier, despite your fine feathers, are less than a man when, exercising your vaunted callousness, you treat peasants as if they were cattle to be slaughtered.'

After this exchange of pleasantries Strabo departed, never to return to the shores of Wales.

Although the campaign was a stalemate and not a defeat, Owain felt that he had been tested and found wanting.

Back in Harlech castle, Owain confided in Young, 'There on Woodbury Hill with the whole of England spread out before me, I realised in my heart that Wales would never be able to muster an army large enough to challenge England's armed might.' He then added bitterly, 'How I wish I had driven Henry down the Severn and into the deep sea, like Arthur did to Twrch Trwyth, the Giant Boar from Hell.'

'Courage, Sire, there is a solution to this, but we will have to act swiftly.'

CHAPTER 12

The Pennal letter

THE VILLAGE OF Pennal lay well south of Harlech and five miles west of Machynlleth. The village contained a particularly fine hall house, Cefn Caer. The house had been built on the site of a former Roman fortress and its pleasant rooms were decorated with historic artefacts discovered on the site. It was to this house that, in March 1406, Chancellor Young brought a troubled Owain Glyn Dŵr. They had one escort, the faithful Madoc ap Gruffydd. The pretext for this flight from Harlech castle was that Owain was in danger of being trapped in the castle by an advancing English army. The real reason lay in Young's plan to restore Owain's credibility. He hoped to persuade the prince to change his allegiance from Pope Boniface in Rome to the alternative Pope Benedict in Avignon. This action would greatly please Charles, who championed Benedict's cause, and would ensure that Owain would soon receive considerably more French military aid than hitherto. The problem was that many of Owain's supporters, especially the Franciscans, considered Benedict to be the Antichrist and would fervently oppose such an action. In Harlech castle, Owain was surrounded by such people led by the fanatical monk Father Huw, and so Young decided to whisk him away to a secret place where he could control access to Owain.

Two who were privy to the location of Owain's secluded sanctuary were Hugh Eddouyer and Maurice Kerry, newly appointed as Owain's envoys to the French court. On March 8th, 1406, they delivered to Owain a letter from Charles in which the King made every effort to persuade Owain to sever the connection with Rome.

★

The tranquillity of life in Cefn Caer, as opposed to the frenetic environment in Harlech castle, and the sweeping views of the surrounding countryside soon restored Owain's spirit. After reading Charles' missive, he listened to Young's plan and endorsed it wholeheartedly. Following detailed discussions it was agreed that Young would draft a letter to Charles informing him of Owain's decision to change his allegiance to Pope Benedict. Owain then decided that a codicil be attached to the letter outlining Owain's vision of an independent Wales and laying down the conditions under which he would recognise Benedict as Pope. Namely, Benedict must withdraw all ecclesiastic censures made against Wales. There must be an independent Church of Wales as a counterpart of an independent principality. St Davids was to be restored to its ancient position as a metropolitan church and would include among its suffragans the bishops of Exeter, Bath, Hereford, Worcester and Lichfield.

At this point, Young protested, 'All those English dioceses! Was ever such a wide claim made before?'

Owain silenced him with, 'You are forgetting the Tripartite Indenture. I am still confident of success beyond the borders of Wales.'

Having written up the codicil, Young then wrote, in Latin, the letter he referred to as the Pennal Letter.

To the most serene and illustrious Prince, Lord Charles, by the grace of God, King of France.

Most Serene Prince, you have deemed it worthy on the humble

*recommendation sent, to learn how my nation, for many years now
elapsed, has been oppressed by the fury of the barbarous Saxons; whence
because they had the government over us, and indeed, on account of the
fact itself, it seemed reasonable with them to trample upon us. But now,
Most Serene Prince, you have in many ways, from your innate goodness,
informed me and my subjects very clearly and graciously concerning the
recognition of the true Vicar of Christ. I, in truth, rejoice with a full
heart on account of that information of Your Excellency, and because,
inasmuch from this information, I understand that the Lord Benedict,
the Supreme Pontifex, intends to work for the promotion of an union in
the Church of God with all his possible strength. Confident indeed in his
right, and intending to agree with you as indeed as far as is possible for
me, I recognise him as the true Vicar of Christ, on my own behalf, and
on behalf of my subjects by these letters patent, foreseeing them by the
bearer of their communications in your majesty's presence. And because,
Most Excellent Prince, the metropolitan church of St David's was, as it
appears, violently compelled by the barbarous fury of those reigning in
this country, to obey the church of Canterbury, and de facto still remains
in this subjection.*

*Many other disabilities are known to have been suffered by the
church of Wales through these barbarians, which for the greater are set
forth fully in the letters patent accompanying. I pray and sincerely beseech
your majesty to have these letters sent to my lord, the supreme pontifex,
that as you deemed worthy to raise us out of darkness into light, similarly
you will wish to extirpate and remove violence and oppression from
the church and from my subjects, as you are well able to. And may the
Son of the Glorious Virgin long preserve your majesty in the promised
prosperity.*

Dated at Pennal the last day of March (1406).
Yours avowedly,
Owain, Prince of Wales.

After re-reading the letter, Young gave a sigh and said to
Owain, 'I do wish you were a little more wholehearted in

acknowledging Benedict as Pope. Why did you insist on entering the caveat "as far as is possible for me"?'

Owain answered impatiently, 'All my instincts tell me that Boniface in Rome is the Vicar of God on this earth. If, to save my rebellion, I must renounce him, so be it. But don't expect me to revel in it.'

Young and Owain both realised that before the letter could be dispatched to Charles it would have to be approved by a conclave of magnates and clerics. Using a device often employed by statesmen who are not confident of being able to secure a majority in full council, Young summoned to Cefn Caer a carefully selected group of like-minded people and obtained the approval he sought. The following morning, Eddouyer and Kerry set out for France bearing the Pennal Letter and its codicil.

As Young and Owain watched the envoys ride into the distance, Young smiled cynically and said, 'I hope they find Charles in a tranquil mood and his wife fully recovered from her recent exertions.'

Owain muttered under his breath, 'It is a sad world when the fate of a proud nation like Wales depends on the mood of a madman.'

★

Charles' response was disappointing and fell far short of Young's expectations. He dispatched twenty-eight ships with a small contingent of troops. Eight of the fleet were captured by the English navy and the remainder deposited on the Welsh coast a thoroughly demoralised group of Frenchmen.

In October, Charles issued a proclamation. Owain and his chancellor eagerly studied the text but found little to celebrate.

'It's no more than an apology for that miserable expedition they sent,' Owain said with disgust, 'embroidered with meaningless expressions of goodwill.'

Young said tartly, 'Your caution at Worcester, when the road to London lay before you, has convinced the French that you will never attempt a full-scale invasion of England.'

Aggrieved, Owain replied, 'Standing there on Woodbury Hill, you agreed that our supply lines were too extended. It was the French who wanted us to attack and advance further into England. That clown Strabo was demanding that we march on London.'

Young answered in a more conciliatory manner, 'Yes Sire, I admit that I and your other advisors were cautious too. But what has exacerbated the situation is the fact that the French realise that the citizens of England have forgotten Richard and are quite content to live under Henry's rule. This has made the French abandon all hope that the population will rise up spontaneously and support us, if we invade England. We can no longer expect significant military aid from them.'

'We still have the Tripartite Indenture and if that fails, then we fight on alone,' Owain growled.

CHAPTER 13

Wales fights best when alone

OWAIN'S BELIEF THAT the Tripartite Indenture would halt the decline in his fortunes suffered a severe blow when news reached him that Northumberland and Bardolf had fled to Scotland to escape Henry's harassment. Despite Young's scepticism, Owain clung to the hope that his exiled allies would be able to raise an army and invade northern England. This last straw was snatched away when, in March 1406, the captain of the guard on the battlements of Harlech castle ordered that the great gate be opened and allowed two weary and dishevelled figures to ride into the castle.

In Owain's chamber, Northumberland and Bardolf told the sad tale of their adventure in Scotland, to a grimfaced Owain and a disbelieving Young.

Northumberland spoke first, 'Never before have I come across such a crude, dour set of lords than those at the court of King Robert.'

Young responded sharply, 'Then why did you seek refuge there? Why did you not come to your Welsh allies, as you do now?'

Northumberland appeared flustered and looked to Bardolf for help.

Bardolf smiled and said wearily, 'Would you have appreciated us arriving at your gates with Henry's army snapping at our heels?'

'Why the sudden departure?' Young asked. 'Was the ambience at the Scottish court too rough for your refined English tastes?'

Bardolf, refusing to lose his temper, replied, 'The cultural climate at the Scottish court leaves much to be desired, as evinced by the fact that King Robert is planning to send his son James to be educated in France. But the sophistication, or lack of it, of our friends across the sea is not the reason for our hasty departure.'

'No indeed!' protested an angry Northumberland. 'No sooner had we settled down among our so-called friends than we discovered that a group of Scottish lords were planning to seize us and exchange us for Scottish prisoners-of-war held by the English.'

Before Young could goad the wretched pair with more questions marinated in cynicism, Owain intervened, 'My friends, our fortunes may appear to be at low ebb and our destiny uncertain...'

Northumberland gave a short, hard laugh.

Owain face darkened and he paused before continuing, 'But our tripartite agreement still stands and now at least we are all together under one roof. This will make it easier to plan the campaigns that lie ahead. As for Scotland, Chancellor Young will seek a rapprochement with King Robert and we'll soon have them back on side.'

As Owain spoke these words, a dramatic encounter was taking place on the high sea. The small vessel which was carrying James to France was intercepted by an English man-of-war, and the heir to the Scottish throne was taken captive. This bad news was compounded when, a month later Robert died, thus making James the King of Scotland.

When reports reached Harlech, Young observed, 'The English now have the advantage of holding the Scottish King as hostage. They will be able to ensure that Scotland will not dare offer us any assistance.'

'I have grown weary of the sporadic help of the French

and the vagaries of the Scots,' Owain growled. 'Wales fights best when it fights alone.'

Young looked sceptical but said nothing.

★

Henry was now three years into his marriage to his second wife Joan of Navarre – a lady who was proving very unpopular and was being blamed for the disfiguring skin complaint that Henry had contracted shortly after the marriage. The tension induced by his unsuccessful attempts to subdue Owain Glyn Dŵr further increased his distress. He decided he never wanted to set foot in Wales again, and, on April 5th, he issued a proclamation, making Prince Hal his deputy in Wales and the Marches. Henry had relinquished control of Wales to his son.

This presented Owain with a new challenge. Up to now he had been able to outwit Henry and send him back over the border like a whipped cur, but young Hal, now grown to manhood, would be a more formidable opponent.

Owain was always in need of revenue to raise and maintain an army in the field – an army of 10,000 to 30,000 men. For this he depended on the pillage and plunder of towns and lordships. He was also able to divert to his own cause the taxes that had once been collected by the English. He was fully aware that the present decline in his military success had dried up this essential flow of income.

Glancing around his chamber at the books and astrological wall charts, he muttered, 'Forget the supernatural, our salvation lies in our military might – the prowess of our bowmen and the sword arms of our warriors.'

He summoned Maredudd and, as the young man entered, Owain gazed with fond concern at Maredudd's elegant but vulnerable body.

'My boy, are you fully recovered from your wounds?'

'Indeed, father, fully recovered,' Maredudd answered cheerfully.

'Then I have a task for you. I want you to lead an army against the English. Believe me, Maredudd, I do not wish to place so great a responsibility on such young shoulders, but I have no option. Gruffydd is a prisoner and Rhys Gethin is slain, and my daughter Catherine would have an attack of the vapours if her precious Edmund strayed more than half a league from the castle.'

Maredudd laughed and said, 'No need for explanations, father. Who better to command Owain Glyn Dŵr's army than his son?'

'It is imperative that we strike the English before Hal has had time to settle into his new role of king's deputy in Wales. When you are on the march send out skirmishers to locate their position and then attack. In a few days I will have mustered a force of 8,000 men. Then will be the time for you to set out.'

Owain clasped Maredudd in a great bear-hug and whispered in his ear, 'May God go with you.'

Long after Maredudd had left the chamber, Owain stood stock-still, a worried frown on his face and tears forming in his eyes.

After one day's march, the scouts reported that a large contingent of the enemy was moving towards them. Despite advice from his captains to proceed with caution, Maredudd ordered an immediate attack only to find that he was heavily outnumbered. The battle ended in a bloodbath with 1,000 Welshmen killed and the rest forced into humiliating flight. It was only then that Maredudd realised that the day he so impetuously attacked the English was April 23rd, St George's Day.

★

In early June, Northumberland and Bardolf took their leave of Owain and, with a small force, set out for north-east Wales, hoping to gain in numbers during their progress. They were, however, intercepted and soundly defeated by Edward Charlton, Lord of Powys, with local musters from Cheshire and Shropshire.

Northumberland and Bardolf escaped but were again faced with the problem of where to seek sanctuary. Louis of Orléans was an implacable enemy of Henry, so the pair scuttled off to France, where they were graciously received by the duke, who lent a sympathetic ear to their plea for military assistance. A man in his early thirties, the Duke of Orléans was the brother of King Charles.

★

In Wales, Owain's situation was becoming desperate. Gower, Towy, Ceredigion and Anglesey had submitted to English rule, but hope remained while Owain still held the castles at Aberystwyth and Harlech.

One summer morning in 1407, the warden of Aberystwyth castle, Rhys Ddu, woke to find Prince Hal camped before the walls of the castle, with a wealth of siege-guns and a large army, among whom were numbered such prominent figures and formidable warriors as the Duke of York and John Talbot. The fall of the castle appeared imminent, but Rhys Ddu was a man of great tactical skill. Watching from the battlements, he noted the casual manner in which Hal's men were setting up the camp. It was obvious that they were not expecting an attack from the castle garrison. Swiftly gathering a tight group of well-armed soldiers, Rhys launched a surprise attack on the besiegers. By the time the enemy had recovered from their shock, Rhys' men had destroyed most of the siege equipment and retreated back into the safety of the castle. Hal was now placed in an embarrassing situation. He could not attack the stout walls of the castle, since he had lost most of his siege equipment, and he was not prepared to make a humiliating retreat. His only option was to negotiate with Rhys Ddu, so, under a flag of truce, Price Hal entered the castle and, after much hard bargaining, an agreement was reached. The terms were carefully delineated: each side agreed to a six week truce, during which both sides would refrain from acts of hostility against each other. At the end of the six week period, Owain Glyn Dŵr would be given one week within which to raise the siege; should he fail, the castle would be delivered intact to the besiegers, while its defenders, after rendering homage to the prince, would be allowed a free pardon and indemnity.

Rhys now had the unenviable task of travelling to Harlech to secure Owain's acquiescence. Owain read the document and raised his eyes to stare in disbelieve and smouldering anger at the unfortunate Rhys.

'Castle will be delivered intact to the besiegers,' Owain roared. 'The defenders, after rending homage to the prince, would be allowed a free pardon.'

Rhys raised his hands in a gesture of helplessness.

Owain continued, 'Having lost Gower, Towy, Ceredigion and Anglesey, have I now sunk so low that I must lose Aberystwyth?'

Rising from his chair he grasped Rhys' shoulders and shouted fully into his face, 'I'm marching to Aberystwyth with the largest force I can muster. You come with me or I'll hang you here on the battlements as a traitor.'

Owain's prompt response, saved the day. Rhys was restored as the warden and Prince Hal was forced into a humiliating retreat.

★

In Paris, Northumberland and Bardolf soon discovered that they had arrived at a time of intense rivalry between Louis and the Duke of Burgundy, who was known as John the Fearless. The cause of this conflict was the fact that Charles' mania had reached the point where he was incapable of ruling France. Louis considered that, as the brother of the afflicted King, he should be Regent. John, however, was a man of unbounded ambition and was determined to make the position his. This situation was resolved by a gruesome murder in a Paris street.

It was a sullen November morning, Louis was riding down rue Vielle du Temple when a gang of assassins burst out of an alleyway and, spreadeagling him across the back of his horse, hacked off both his arms before piercing his defenceless body with their rapiers. John boasted that he had hired the men and brazenly stated, 'It was a justifiable act of tyranny.'

This act brought France to the brink of civil war and so alarmed Northumberland and Bardolf that they fled to Scotland, with the highly optimistic intention of raising an army for the invasion of England. But the Scots, painfully aware that their King was held captive by Henry, would have nothing to do with the undertaking. Northumberland and Bardolf were reduced to recruiting criminals and the destitute, who felt that life in an army of insurrection could not be worse than the life they were already suffering.

When the rag, tag and bobtail army crossed the border and headed for York, Northumberland sent a message to Owain, beleaguered in his castle at Harlech, begging him to join them in an attack on York. The messenger, concerned for Owain's welfare, intimated the poor quality of Northumberland's men and how during the march they had picked up very few volunteers. Owain, brooding in his chamber with the faithful Madoc at the door, thought back to the occasions when he had received similar requests – Richard at Flint and Hotspur at Shrewsbury. Each time he had let his mind rule his heart and refused. Realising that his decision would mean the end of the Tripartite Indenture, he sent the messenger back with a letter wishing Northumberland success but informing him that Owain Glyn Dŵr was in no position to assist him.

★

On February 19th, the rebels reached Bramham Moor, south of Wetherby. The winter was one of great severity and the ground was a vast carpet of frozen snow. On reading Owain's message, Northumberland realised, for the first time how his son Hotspur must have felt on learning that his father was not coming to join him at Shrewsbury. The letter fell from his hand and was blown away in the howling winter wind. Northumberland's scouts reported that a force of Yorkshire levies, under the command of Sir Thomas Rokeby, High Sheriff of Yorkshire, was advancing to confront them. Northumberland stationed his men and waited for Rokeby's arrival. It was two o'clock in the afternoon when battle commenced. Rokeby had his longbow men subject the rebels to a period of withering fire before he ordered a charge by his main force. The battle then degenerated into a confused mêlée in the centre of the field. Northumberland's small force was wiped out, and he died fighting a furious rearguard action. Thus ended the Percy family's challenge to the legitimacy of Henry's coronation. His fellow rebel, Bardolf, died of his wounds shortly after the battle and, much to the distress of his widow, his body was quartered and the parts were disposed of by being placed above the gates of London, York, Lincoln and Shrewsbury. Lincoln was further honoured by being given his severed head. Bardolf's widow, a woman of great determination, so pestered Prince Hal that he granted her permission to gather up the parts of her husband's body and give them a Christian burial.

When news of Northumberland's demise reached Westminster, Henry mumbled sadly, 'This Percy was the man nearest my soul who, like a brother, toiled in my affairs and laid his love under my foot. That it should come to this, that I rejoice in his slaying. Are these things then necessities?'

Prince Hal annoyed by his father's maudlin reaction, said harshly, 'If they are, by the nature of man, then let us meet them like necessities. Northumberland proved false to Richard then grew to a greater falseness against you. He deserved no better death.'

★

Maredudd now took on the role of receiving all the reports, mainly discouraging, that flooded into the castle from Owain's spies. He analysed and moderated these before passing them on to Owain.

'News that Adam arrived at Barmouth a week ago,' Maredudd said casually.

'Adam?' Owain questioned.

'Adam of Usk, that ambitious cleric who changes his allegiances more frequently than his shirt. Went from a teaching post in Oxford to serve Richard and then became a member of the commission that found legal grounds for the deposition of his former patron. Prospered under Henry but then forfeited the King's favour by his aggressive behaviour and was forced to flee to Rome.'

'Charged with highway robbery,' Owain mused. 'Though I find it hard to believe that.'

'Riots in Rome made him move to Bruges and he was tempted to join Northumberland in his rebellion against

Henry but, when the time came for action, he avoided any involvement.'

'That could be said of us,' Owain averred. 'What's he doing landing at Barmouth?'

'I believe he thought of joining us but, now that our fortunes are in decline, I doubt you'll be seeing him.'

'No, he'll make his way to Usk and seek the protection of his native lord, Edward Charlton. He'll then apply for the King's pardon.'

'A man for all seasons our Adam.'

Owain sighed and said, 'To be charitable, these are difficult times when fortunes fluctuate so tortuously.'

★

At this low point in Owain's fortunes, David Gam decided it was time to extinguish forever the pretensions of the rebel prince. He mustered a compact force of well-armed soldiers and headed straight for Harlech. He believed that Owain's credibility had been so damaged by these recent reverses that the garrison would desert Owain and surrender the castle.

When Owain was informed by his spies that his bitterest foe was approaching, expecting the castle to fall to his small determined force, he summoned Maredudd.

'Gam is heading our way,' Owain said, 'so confident of an easy victory that he has brought an insultingly small troop.'

Maredudd laughed, 'These stout walls will have no difficulty in keeping him out.'

'I think we can take advantage of his arrogance and lay him by the heels. You remember the ruse by which we captured Lord Grey? At Ruthin, we were the besiegers. Here we will be the besieged so we reverse the strategy. When he arrives we open the gate and once he enters we shut them, with most of his men still outside. We'll have him like a rat in a trap.'

'But will he be so stupid as to fall for so obvious a trick?'

'Hatred such as his induces blindness.'

Gam appeared before the gate of Harlech castle astride a magnificent white stallion. Behind him, also mounted, were the grim visaged men of his squadron.

Gam arrogantly shouted up to the guards on the battlements, 'The King's pardon, if you open the gate and yield up the traitor Owain Glyn Dŵr.'

At a signal from Owain, who was standing in the courtyard, the guards swung the great doors open.

Gam rode boldly in, but before the majority of his men were able to follow him, Owain cried, 'Close the gates.'

The few soldiers that had entered were swiftly surrounded and disarmed. Gam realised that he had been tricked and in fury he leapt from his horse and, brandishing a long-bladed dagger, flung himself upon Owain. Despite the passing of the years, Owain still had the upper body strength that had broken the back of Hywel Sele and hurled him into a hollow tree stump. Owain easily tore the dagger from Gam's hand and crushed the breath from his body before contemptuously throwing him to the floor. Madoc raised his fearsome axe and was about to bring it crashing down on Gam's twitching figure.

'No!' Owain ordered. 'He will be more use alive than dead. Bind him securely and carry him into the castle.'

That evening, guided by the light of a rush candle, Owain made his way to the room where Gam was chained to the wall. As he entered, Gam sprang towards him but fell back with a grunt of pain as the chains restrained him.

Standing well clear of the infuriated creature, Owain said calmly, 'Be at peace, I have not come to harm you but to reason with you.'

Gam snarled, 'I have given you reason enough to harm me a thousand times over.'

140

'I would far rather find out why you have committed these atrocities against your own people. You are a Welshman, I presume.'

'I can claim as ancient a Welsh lineage as yours. The line stretches far back to the kings of Brycheiniog.'

'That makes it even harder to understand your hatred of the Welsh.'

Gam said impatiently, 'I'm not motivated by hatred of the Welsh but by loyalty to the English crown. My family have always been faithful supporters of the de Bohun family and have prospered under an English hegemony. Were your rebellion to succeed that authority would be destroyed and chaos would reign.'

'For all your talk of political motivation, I feel you harbour a personal hatred for me. Why?'

'I beheaded three hundred of your men at Usk in retribution for your callous murder of my friend and mentor Hywel Sele.'

Owain stared thoughtfully at Gam and said almost in a whisper, 'It's a terrible thing to hold the power of life and death over another person. All here will urge me to avenge the atrocities you have committed by subjecting you to the most painful death imaginable. I wonder what King Henry would do if you attempted to bury your knife in him? I must have time to think this out.'

'He would send me a goblet of wine and fine food and have it placed beyond my grasp.'

Owain turned and, walking towards the door, said, 'I will see that you get fresh water and food every day.'

Owain did consult with his followers but, despite their unanimous demand that Gam be put to death, he decided to ransom his captive and set the price at an exorbitant 500 marks. Gam's worth to the English cause was soon made manifest when Henry, with surprising alacrity, made the money available. Before Owain released Gam, he made him vow that he would never again take up arms against Owain's cause. He then unlocked the iron collar around Gam's neck and let the chains crash to the ground.

Gam gazed, a little bemused, at Owain and asked, 'Why?'

Owain answered, 'If you're asking why I ransomed you instead of killing you, the answer is simple – I needed the money. I know that the oath you have just sworn means nothing to you and you will be back whispering in Henry's ear as soon as you leave this cell.'

'I ask again. Why are you doing this?'

'Because, looking to the future, I can see death close on your heels.'

Well aware of Owain's reputation as a wizard, Gam's face turned white.

★

Crach Ffinnant, called the Scab because of his disfigurement, had been Owain's chief bard since the death of Iolo Goch. Throughout this period he had been a loyal servant to Owain, composing eulogistic ballads to commemorate Owain's triumphs. However, in view of Owain's recent defeats, the Scab's faith in Owain's ability to attain the ultimate victory was fatally undermined. He began to spread the word among the garrison that Owain should be removed from the leadership and replaced by someone more decisive. When asked who this person might be, he answered that one of the Tudor brothers from Ynys Môn would fit the bill.

This uncharacteristic behaviour had a deep psychological cause. The Scab nursed a burning desire to possess Alice, Walter Brut's widow, but the realisation that his facial disfigurement ruled out all hope of his love ever being requited so infuriated the Scab that it warped his mind and he resolved to murder Alice and, in the resulting confusion, encompass Owain's downfall.

The Scab, being the Bard of Derfel, knew that in the past, a tribe on the eve of battle would enact a religious ceremony. They would choose a maiden and take her to Derfel's shrine at Llanderfel as a symbolic 'Bride of Derfel'. This ritual provided the means by which the Scab would be able to carry out his foul purpose. He approached Alice and, ignoring her icy disdain, announced that he was organising a pilgrimage to Derfel's shrine, which lay a good day's march from Harlech. Alice's first reaction was to dismiss the idea, but she had heard rumours that the Scab had been fermenting dissention among the soldiers. So, in order to discover more, she consented. As soon as the Scab left her, she hurried to Owain's study and reported what had occurred. Owain listened carefully to what she said and then informed her that he was well aware of Crach Ffinnant's eccentric behaviour. He fastidiously avoided using the offensive sobriquet Scab. Owain, anxious not to place Alice in danger, told her not to accompany Ffinnant to the shrine, but Alice countered by saying that it was of the utmost importance that they learn more of the Scab's intentions. Reluctantly Owain agreed but insisted that Maredudd accompany her at all times. Before she left, Owain kissed her right hand and was disturbed to discover that his heart started to thump. He had not yet succeeded in eradicating the mythical illusions associated with Brut's widow.

The following morning a small mounted party of pilgrims set out for the shrine at Llanderfel: Crach Ffinnant, Alice, Maredudd, Catherine, Edmund and an escort of four soldiers. The light was failing when, after a long journey over the mountains, the group reached the church at Llanderfel. The shrine was situated inside the church, but when Maredudd attempted to accompany Alice into the church, his way was barred by a determined Crach Ffinnant.

'The only one to conduct the Bride of Derfel to the shrine is the Bard of Derfel,' Ffinnant said firmly.

When the others protested, Ffinnant warned, 'If the correct ritual is not observed, disaster will befall the house of Owain Glyn Dŵr.'

Ffinnant and Alice entered the church alone. It was the first time Alice had set eyes on the wooden statue of Derfel and his great horse. The first thing that struck her was its enormous size and garish paintwork, Derfel's eyes appeared to glow like balls of fire. While she stood overawed by the spectacle, she became aware that Ffinnant was creeping up behind her. She had come prepared for this moment and as he sprang upon her clutching a dagger in his right-hand, Alice drew from under her tunic a vicious long-bladed knife and, holding it in two hands, thrust it skilfully through his ribs and into his heart. The Scab died instantly and Alice lugged the corpse out of the church and deposited it at the feet of a startled Maredudd. When the group started back for Harlech, Alice rode proudly in front with the body of the Scab strapped across the back of her horse.

On her return, she calmly said to Owain, 'He was a constant danger to you and your great cause. It was a deed that had to be done.'

Before Owain could reply, Alice turned and swiftly left the room, leaving Owain torn by two conflicting emotions – admiration for her courage and the shock he felt at the cold-blooded nature of her disposition.

CHAPTER 14

Owain becomes an outlaw

ENCOURAGED BY THE English victory at Bramham Moor, Prince Hal launched an onslaught on Aberystwyth and Harlech, Owain's only remaining power bases in Wales.

Aberystwyth castle, despite Owain's bold action in the summer of 1407, was the first to capitulate. Chancellor Young was forced to scamper to safety in a manner not commensurate with what he perceived as the dignity of his office.

When he arrived at Harlech castle, Owain dismissed his grumbles with the words, 'The way things look at the moment, you had better prepare to clamber down the seaward wall as Hal comes marching in through the gates.'

However, Harlech, standing majestically on its lofty crag, was to prove a far more difficult proposition. Owain was fully aware that not only did Harlech castle harbour the members of his family, but it was now the sole remaining fortress under his command. Lose it and he would become a guerrilla fighting in the forests and moorland.

Speaking in the great hall, he exhorted the garrison, 'Sons of Ardudwy, that fertile swathe of land stretching from Barmouth to the walls of this castle, defend the heritage of King Bendigeidfran, who held his court here at Harlech. When he was slain in the war against the Irish, his severed head was returned to Harlech where it was retained for seven years protecting the castle, until it was taken to London. It is said that the head was able to speak and entertained the garrison with his tales from ancient mythology.'

Young whispered in Maredudd's ear, 'He became such a

garrulous bore, they packed him off to the island of Gwales for 80 years and then to London, where he immediately fell silent.'

'If you ask me,' Maredudd said, 'he was himself part of that mythology.'

The besieging force was led by Gilbert Talbot of Goodrich and his brother John. One of their main difficulties was the provision of supplies. The fate of John Horne, a wholesale fishmonger of London, was typical of the tradesmen who supplied the besiegers. While attempting to discharge a cargo of fish, he was attacked by the garrison, who seized his goods, burnt his ship and held him to ransom.

The men of Ardudwy defended resolutely but it became obvious to Owain that the persistent and savage cannonading, from the great guns brought from York, was reducing sections of the stout walls of the mighty fortress to rubble. In addition, Hal's longbow men were thinning the ranks of the defenders with deadly accuracy. In a council of war, it was decided that certain important items should be smuggled out of the castle. These included sensitive diplomatic papers and a velvet bag that contained a golden helmet, cuirass and sword – the gift that Charles had sent to Owain. It was also agreed that when defeat was imminent, Owain, together with Maredudd, Madoc, Young and Edmund, would attempt to descend the sea wall and escape by boat. It was felt that the women of Owain's household would not possess the necessary physical strength and dexterity to survive the hazardous descent of the sea wall. Also it was thought that their rank would ensure that they would be treated courteously by their captors. However, when Owain visited the women's quarters and informed them of the council's decision, the Arglwyddes and Catherine demanded that Edmund must stay behind and ensure that they were not abused by their English captors. Alice, dressed in a black leather tunic and breaches, coolly informed Owain that she was as capable as any man and would prefer to take her chance with the escapees than be captured by the English. Remembering her history and her recent exploits, Owain concurred.

★

On his way to the escape route, Owain saw a horse's harness lying discarded on the stone paving stones. He stooped, and, gathering it up, studied the gilt bronze boss bearing the four lions rampant.

He showed the boss to Maredudd, who was at his side, and said wistfully, 'The four lions rampant that I had emblazoned on my banner when I assumed the title Prince of Wales. Will this small boss be the only thing that I will leave to posterity from all the greatness that was once Owain Glyn Dŵr?'

Fighting back the tears gathering in his eyes, Maredudd whispered, 'Courage father, our cause is not lost.'

The escape party, with the exception of Young, had little difficulty in abseiling the seaward wall and clambering aboard the small vessel that would take them a few miles down the coast to safety. Madoc, with his ever-present murderous axe tucked in his belt, led the way. Alice made the descent with the agility of a sleek panther. Chancellor Young, with flailing arms and legs, fell into the sea and had to be hauled, gasping like a hooked fish, out of the water.

Within the castle, the women had taken refuge in the Roland tower, and Edmund with sword in hand stood guard at the entrance, determined to let no man enter until he was assured of the women's safety. When the English flooded into the castle, poor Edmund Mortimer was swept from his post and hacked to pieces. The Arglwyddes, Catherine and her three daughters by Edmund were taken captive and transported unceremoniously to London.

Watching, from the bow of his boat, the capitulation of his last stronghold in Wales, Owain murmured, 'I am as a deposed king cowering on a rain-ravished moor bemoaning my fate to a howling wind.'

'No father,' Maredudd cried. 'I see you as a lion in winter on the snow-capped heights of Snowdon, cold and hungry in that alien landscape but fiercely stalking your prey.'

'A lion on Snowdon?' Owain chuckled. 'Oh Maredudd, you have such an imagination.'

Flinging out his arms, Owain pressed his son to his breast.

★

Owain realised that his rebellion had now entered a phase of what he thought of as irregular warfare, in which his small group of warriors, lacking any form of secure base camp, would have to employ mobile military tactics involving ambushes and raids to combat a larger but less mobile army.

He recalled Young's phrase, "more strategy and less gymnastics" and murmured, 'We are going to need more strategy and even more gymnastics.'

On landing he sent out commands to all those still loyal to him to assemble at Sycharth. Although this once elegant mansion was now a total ruin, it would provide some temporary shelter for his beleaguered band. When Owain and his immediate entourage arrived at Sycharth, he was encouraged to discover many of his most faithful supporters had answered his call. Among them were: Bishop John Trevor, Philip Hanmer, Henry Don, Rhys Ddu, Rhys and Ednyfed of Penmynydd. They had brought a gratifying number of armed men with them.

Now was the time for Owain to inspire these demoralised men and there, in the roofless hall of his former home, he stood on a shattered piece of masonry and addressed his followers. 'We have no fortified castle as a base and so will not be able to fight a regular war. Our rebellion has entered a new stage, that of irregular warfare. Violence is not the prerogative of the exploiters, the exploited can use it, too. I am not advocating passive self-defence, but defence with attack. Its final goal is the conquest of political power. We must not turn from violence, it is the midwife of new societies.'

This rather incoherent jumble of esoteric ideas puzzled the majority of his listeners. It was not the inspirational speech they had expected and longed for.

Aware of this, Owain tried again. 'Each of you is a freedom fighter par excellence, the people's choice in their struggle for liberation. We are a pure army that resists the temptations common to men through our rigid consciousness of duty and discipline.'

His audience was still unmoved and a voice rang out, 'What is left?'

Young stepped forward, and spoke in less abstruse terms, 'You might well ask the question, What is left? I'll tell you what we have left. We have the spirit of an indomitable leader and an army that is not daunted by adversity. Together they will liberate this land from the yoke of the English.'

His words ignited the assembly, the soldiers cheered and stamped their feet. Owain smiled ruefully, it had taken a priest to find the phrases that would excite a crowd of warriors – 'indomitable leader… not daunted by adversity… the English yoke.'

Encouraged by his reception, Young continued, 'We band of marauders shall so harass the Marcher lords that they will fear for their land and for the lives of their families.'

Owain, feeling it was time to reassert his authority, said, 'We are not alone in this struggle. The people of Wales are on our side and will assist us in living off the land. There are still strong contingents of Scottish rebels among our ranks and many French men have chosen to remain here. Furthermore my chancellor, Griffith Young, will be going on a mission to France and will, with God's help, return with reinforcements. Courage, brothers in arms, victory is there to be seized just as Jason snatched the Golden Fleece from the sacred grove under the watchful eye of the white dragon.'

His words were brave and defiant but in his heart he dreaded the adversity that lay ahead. The loss of Harlech was more than a military setback; it meant that he could no longer claim to be a creditable ruling prince. He had become, at a stroke, a hunted outlaw whose wife and family had been taken as captives to London.

★

That night, Owain, wrapped in his cloak, settled down under the shelter of one of Sycharth's crumbling walls. Madoc, his bodyguard, lay near him.

CHAPTER 15

From Ambrosius to Arthur

T HE NATURE OF the warfare they now waged – making a swift assault on a town and then beating a hasty retreat – meant that at night they were forced to make camp in forests or open fields, vulnerable to a surprise attack. This necessitated guards being placed all around the camp. Owain insisted that he played his part and so he and Madoc spent many a dark night patrolling the boundaries of the encampment. During one of these patrols, Madoc asked Owain to continue with the history of the kings of Briton.

Owain felt a flush of pride at Madoc's request and resumed the story, 'After Vortigern's death, Ambrosius was crowned King but his court was thrown into panic when news arrived that Hengist had assembled a massive army of Saxons on the Scottish border.

'When asked how he was going to deal with the situation, Ambrosius answered, "By forming an army larger than his, and marching north to destroy him and his Saxons."

'In his march north, Ambrosius passed through lands that had been devastated by the Saxons. He wept and vowed that he would exact a terrible punishment on Hengist for the desolation he had caused. Hengist, gathering his men around him, exhorted them to have courage. "I speak to every man here," he declaimed. "Do not fear these Britons. Have you not defeated them time and time again? Have you not, time after time, left the battlefield bloody but victorious? Courage, courage! I solemnly swear victory will be yours."

'Having emboldened his men, Hengist marched to meet

Ambrosius. Hengist knew that Ambrosius would have to pass through a large flat field surrounded by gently sloping hills. It was there that he planned to ambush Ambrosius and fall upon the Britons when they were least expecting it. However a spy informed Ambrosius of the plan, so that, when the Saxons reached the field, Ambrosius had his men drawn up in full battle order and ready to fight.

'When the two armies met face to face, Ambrosius challenged Hengist to single combat. Now, Ambrosius was a man of magnificent physical presence: the powerful limbs, the noble head and the aura of majesty. In single combat he always dashed his opponent from his horse and left him dead upon the ground, while he rode off in triumph brandishing his splintered lance. Hengist was greatly frightened and declined the offer.'

'I'm not surprised, he had every reason to be terrified,' Madoc commented with a chuckle.

'Before the battle commenced, Eldol, one of Ambrosius' knights, went to the King and said, "I would consider this one day a sufficient recompense for all the remaining days of my life, if God would grant that I may fight hand-to-hand with Hengist, for one of us would die as we attacked each other with our swords."

'Ambrosius asked, "Why this personal antagonism?"

'"Once before the commencement of a battle, I sent three unarmed men under the flag of truce to parley with Hengist and the villain stuck a knife into each one of them."

'Eldol made his challenge but Hengist scornfully rejected it. The time had come for Ambrosius to address his army. "Britons!" he cried. "Fight as one for our homeland and attack the enemy boldly. God fights at our side and we cannot fail."

'The Britons moved forward in a determined attack on

the Saxons and both armies became involved in savage close-order combat. All around could be heard the grunts of men desperately fighting for their lives, and the groans of the dying. In the course of the battle, Eldol and Hengist came face to face and began to rain blows on each other. As each in turn slashed with his sword, the sparks flew but neither could unhorse the other. Then Eldol grasped Hengist by the helmet and dragged him to the ground, where the Britons bound him fast. A great floodtide of joy boiled up within Eldol and he shouted, "God has answered my prayer. Now that Hengist has been captured the enemy will flee. Victory is ours."

'Ambrosius led one final charge against the Saxons and drove them from the field. Once the victory was secured, Ambrosius demonstrated his compassion. He ordered that the dead be buried and the wounded receive medical attention, friend and foe alike. When Hengist stood before him, Ambrosius felt pity for his defeated enemy and would have spared his life, but Eldol and others demanded that Hengist be killed. Reluctantly the King gave his consent and Eldol dispatched him with a mighty blow from his sword. Ambrosius ordered Hengist's body to be buried and a barrow of earth be raised over his body, that being the pagan way.

'Ambrosius now proved to be a wise and benevolent King. He spent his time travelling from city to city restoring all the buildings that the Saxons had destroyed. When he came to the monastery at Salisbury, the monks told him that on that spot were buried many of the leaders and princes who had died nobly defending their fatherland. "Such men," Ambrosius declared, "are worthy of a memorial that will stand for ever and be one of the wonders of the world. Who is the architect capable of building such an edifice?"

'The monks answered immediately, "The only man here

who has the ability to carry out your plan is the prophet Merlin."

'"Merlin, of course. Bring him to me."

'On being told the task, Merlin said, "If you wish to grace the burial place of these noble men, you must obtain the Giant's Ring which is on Mount Killaraus in Ireland. It is constructed out of enormous stones that no man can move. It is said that it was erected by the gods and will stand for ever."

'"If what you say is true, how do you plan to achieve such an impossible task?" Ambrosius asked.

'Merlin answered, "Give me the support of the finest of your fighting men, for the Irish will defend their sacred edifice with their lives. Then leave the rest to me."

'Crossing the Irish sea, Merlin and his escort fought through determined resistance to Mount Killaraus, where they gazed up in awe at the Giant's Ring.

'Ambrosius exclaimed, "We will never be able to remove those stones and take them to Salisbury, they are far too large and heavy."

'Merlin smiled and started, in a low mystical voice, to chant an ancient spell. The sky became dark as the sun was obscured by the wings of a thousand gyrating black eagles. As the army looked on in amazement, the birds plucked up the massive stones as if they were mere pebbles and flew swiftly away.

'When Ambrosius recovered from the shock, he asked, "Where have the eagles taken the stones?"

'Merlin answered, "Having flown across the sea to Salisbury, they are now building the Giant's Ring on the site ordained by you."

'Merlin had spoken the truth, for when the soldiers returned to Britain they found the Giant's Ring towering above the tallest spires in the city, and the people speaking excitedly of the great black eagles that assembled it.

'For many years, Ambrosius ruled the kingdom with justice and his people were content, but there was one man whose heart was bursting with hatred for Ambrosius. His name was Paschent and he was the son of Vortigern, who had died at the hands of Ambrosius and his brother Uther Pendragon. His one desire was to avenge the death of his father.

'One day a Saxon, called Eopa, came to Paschent and asked, "How much will you give the man who kills Ambrosius for you?"

'"If only I could find a man who was prepared to do that," answered Paschent, "I would give him a fortune in silver and my friendship for as long as I lived. Also, if I became King, I would make him the captain of my bodyguard."

'Eopa was pleased. "I have heard it said that Ambrosius is suffering from a slight fever. If you will fulfil what you have promised, then I will disguise myself as a Briton and gain admittance to the King by pretending to be a doctor. I will then mix for him a poisonous potion that will kill him."

'Carrying a load of pots filled with medicines, Eopa journeyed to Winchester, where Ambrosius was lying ill, and offered his services to the King's retainers. No one could have been more welcome than a doctor and they led him to the King.

'Eopa then prepared a deadly poison and handed it to Ambrosius telling him to drink it down in one gulp. This the King did and then settled down to sleep, imagining that he would recover his health. The poison ran quickly through his veins and death came as he slept. The assassin Eopa slipped away in the crowd.

'Uther Pendragon hurried down from the north to be

present at his brother's funeral. The whole nation mourned the death of their beloved King. As they laid him to rest within the Giant's Ring, there appeared a star of great magnitude and brilliance, with a single beam of light shining from it. At the end of this beam was the shape of a fiery dragon. The people were greatly perturbed and asked Merlin to tell them what the star portended.

'Merlin stood up before the mourners and said, "Our loss is irreparable. Our most illustrious King has been taken from us. Ambrosius, King of the Britons, has been murdered and by his death we shall die, unless God brings us help."

'Merlin turned to Uther Pendragon and spoke directly to him, "Hasten forward, Uther Pendragon, and accept the throne. God has chosen you to be the saviour of your people. That is the meaning of the star that is not a star. It is a comet and has been sent by God."

'Uther knelt before Merlin and said, "I submit to the will of God."

'Merlin placed the crown on Uther Pendragon's head and declaimed, "I crown you King of all Britain. Arise King Uther Pendragon."

'Uther rose to the cheers of the people and declared, "Before I can lay claim to being the King of all Britain, I must drive the Saxon invaders from our fair land."

'This he proceeded to do without delay. Gathering as large an army as he could, he marched north to face Paschent and his Saxon warriors. As soon as the two armies came within sight of each other they drew up their lines of battle and marched forward to make contact, and so the battle began. As happens in such a combat, many soldiers were slain on both sides. At the end of the day Uther proved the stronger and won the victory, killing Paschent in the process. The Saxons turned and fled to their ships.

'Uther then turned his attention to Octa, the son of the slain Hengist. This Saxon lord put himself at the head of a large army of bloodthirsty Saxons and invaded the north of England, laying waste many towns and strong points. Uther gathered together the whole might of the kingdom and went in pursuit of Octa. He caught up with Octa when he was besieging York. The Saxons manfully resisted Uther's assaults and then drove the Britons back in flight. They pursued the Britons as far as Mount Damen then halted because night fell and there was no light to see by. Mount Damen was a steep hill and on its summit it had a wood, while halfway up there was a crop of jagged rocks.

'The Britons occupied the hill and Uther called his officers together in a council of war. Uther asked Gorlois, the Duke of Cornwall, a man of great experience to give his views on their perilous situation.

'"This is no moment," said Gorlois, "for idle chatter. While some remnant of light remains, we must act boldly and bravely if we expect to enjoy either life or liberty. The Saxons outnumber us and, if we wait until dawn, we will be massacred. Let us make our move while darkness lasts. We must clamber down in close formation and surprise them in their camp. We shall triumph only if we attack them in the boldest possible fashion, for they will not have foreseen anything of this sort."

'While Gorlois was speaking, Uther was eyeing the duke with great suspicion, as if he thought that at some time in the future Gorlois might challenge him for the crown. Uther hid his suspicions and said, "The advice that Gorlois gives well pleases me. We will put it into operation immediately."

'As soon as they were armed and drawn up into companies, they set off down the mountain, scrambling through the rocks. When they reached the enemy camp, they charged forward with drawn swords and routed the Saxons. Octa was captured and Uther ordered that he be imprisoned for the rest of his life.

'Uther now ruled his kingdom with justice but those who committed crimes were punished mercilessly. One day word came to Uther that Gorlois was planning a rebellion. Uther had long suspected that Gorlois was not a faithful subject and had designs on the crown. He acted with ruthless efficiency, and marched down to Cornwall at the head of a large army and laid siege to the fortress of Tintagel, where Gorlois had taken refuge. Uther summoned Merlin and asked his advice on how best to enter the castle.

'Merlin replied, "As you can see the castle is built high above the sea, which surrounds it on all sides. There is no other way in except that offered by a narrow strip of rock. Three armed soldiers could hold that against you no matter how many men you had."

'"Can nothing be done?" Uther demanded.

'"Wait until dusk," Merlin replied.

'As the evening crept in, Merlin and Uther stood looking across the raging sea at the battlements of Tintagel. Behind them stood the serried ranks of Uther's army.

'Merlin raised his arms in supplication and started to chant an ancient spell. As the chanting grew louder, a large white cloud appeared against the darkening sky. It slowly moved until it formed a bridge from where Merlin stood to the battlements of the castle. "There," Merlin said in triumph, march your army across the bridge and Tintagel will be yours."

'"Are you mad," Uther shouted. "How can an army march on a cloud?"

'Merlin laughed and said, "Like this." He grabbed Uther's hand and they both started to walk on the cloud. Uther was amazed to discover that the surface of the cloud was as firm as the solid earth. He gave the order and the army marched swiftly across the cloud bridge and stormed the castle. In the fighting the castle was taken and the traitorous Gorlois was slain. For the first time, Uther felt secure on his throne.

'Uther Pendragon lived for many years and fought valiantly to protect Britain from the Saxons. After his last great victory over the Saxons he fell ill and was carried to the town of St Albans to recuperate. Near the royal residence was a spring of limpid water which the King used to drink. His enemies learnt of this and polluted the spring with poison. When Uther drank a goblet of the contaminated water, he died immediately. And that was the last of Uther.'

Madoc appeared to be quite affected by Owain's account of Uther's life and cruel death.

'Cheer up Madoc,' Owain cried. 'The best is yet to come, Arthur and the fellowship of the Round Table. But dawn is breaking and brings with it a sea of troubles.'

★

The next time they were on guard duty, Owain continued the narrative. 'The death of Uther Pendragon so encouraged the Saxons that they overran many areas of Briton in an attempt to exterminate the Britons. Alarmed, Merlin called an assembly of the lords of Briton. They met at the town of Silchester and their urgent task was to elect a new king. Merlin, as if from a hat, produced a fifteen-year-old youth, Arthur, whom he claimed was a direct descendent of Uther Pendragon. If the truth be known, when Uther laid siege to Tintagel, the fortress was not the only thing that fell to his assault. It was know that he lusted after Ygerna, the beautiful wife of the traitor Gorlois.

'When Merlin proposed that the assembly elect Arthur as their king, there were cries of, "How can this child be our king? Merlin is mocking us all."

'Merlin then laid his hand on the youth's shoulder and commanded, "Kneel before Arthur the Once and Future King of Britain."

'To Arthur's amazement, the unruly crowd obeyed and thus Britain acquired its greatest king. Arthur gathered many good knights around him and defeated the Saxons, so that the land was at peace. Then, under Merlin's guidance, Arthur set up his Round Table at Camelot.'

'Why did he make the table round?'

'So that all should be equal, for none could have a higher place at a table which was round. When King Arthur and his knights rode forth, dead flowers bloomed again and the withered branches on dying trees blossomed once more.

'Arthur took to wife Guinevere, the descendent of a noble Roman family and the most beautiful woman in the land. For many years King Arthur and his knights defended Briton from the Picts, the Scots, the Irish and the Saxons. Then dissention within the fellowship of the Round Table brought about the end of Arthur's reign. While Arthur was away attacking Rome, his cousin Mordred openly lived adulterously with Guinevere and attempted to usurp the throne. Arthur fought his last battle on the plain of Camlann, against the evil Sir Mordred. After many hours the field of battle was strewn with the bodies of slaughtered knights. Arthur was resting on the ground with his back against a tree, blood flowing from his many wounds. Mordred suddenly appeared out of the thick mist that was creeping over the battlefield. With a howl of rage Arthur, springing to his feet, picked up a bronze-tipped lance and charged at the knight who by his evil machinations had destroyed the communion of the Round Table. Mordred struck Arthur a powerful blow across his helmet but Arthur, undeterred, thrust his lance through Mordred's shield and breastplate until it skewered his heart. Mordred lay dead at Arthur's feet. Arthur, knowing he was mortally wounded, asked his knights to carry him to the shore where there floated a barge, the rowers were young maidens dressed in long cloaks and hoods of the deepest black. They placed Arthur in the boat and with much weeping the maidens rowed from the land to the magic vale of Avalon.'

Madoc asked, 'Where he died, I suppose?'

'Some believe to this day that Arthur is still alive and that, in a secret cave in the mountains of Snowdonia, he sleeps surrounded by his knights. When Britain is in dire danger, they will wake from their sleep, don their armour and answer Britain's call.'

'Do you believe that?'

Owain chuckled and said, 'Many more believe that Arthur sprang from a family of Romans that remained in Briton after the great exodus of AD 410 and that we Welsh are nothing more than a nation of Roman bastards.'

CHAPTER 16

The death of Owain's golden vision

OWAIN STILL HAD a significant following and, aided by the French and Scots, was able to inflict devastation throughout Wales, by random lightning raids on unprepared English settlements. The anxiety this caused Henry became evident when a party of horsemen under a flag of truce appeared outside Owain's fortified camp. Even from a distance, Owain recognised the gargantuan figure of Sir John Oldcastle. In the privacy of Owain's tent, the two old friends embraced.

Oldcastle was the first to speak. 'I come from Henry…'

'Of course, from whom else?' quipped Owain.

'Owain, listen to what I have to say. I bring the one chance you have of surviving this conflict. Henry offers you and all your followers a pardon if you lay down your arms and become faithful subjects of the English crown.'

'John, go back to Henry and tell him that Owain Glyn Dŵr will never bend a knee to an English monarch, no matter if he comes festooned with pardons.'

'Listen to me, Owain…'

'Enough! We will speak of this no more.'

Owain paused and asked tentatively, 'Have you news of my daughter Alys?'

Oldcastle appeared disconcerted by the question and chose his words with care. 'She was very happy at Almeley where no one suspected that she was your daughter. I had let it be known that she was the daughter of a distant cousin of mine. One day I entertained a young man who was the warden of Carreg Cennen castle near Llandeilo and the son of a substantial Herefordshire family.'

Owain interrupted Oldcastle, 'John Scudamore, his name was John Scudamore.'

'Well, yes.'

'He defended the castle against my siege but what does he have to do with my daughter?'

'You know young people, they liked each other's company and to cut a long story short, they are now married and living at Monnington Straddel in the Golden Valley, Herefordshire.'

'Does he know she is my daughter?'

'Yes, but no one else. If known, it would compromise his position in the King's service.'

Owain lent back in his chair and closed his eyes.

In a voice heavy with emotion Owain intoned, 'My wife and family prisoners in the Tower; my daughter Alys married to an officer in the service of Henry. The elegant home Sycharth, with its moat, tiled roofs, tall chimneys, deer park and mill, where we all lived so happily, now reduced to a derelict jumble of fallen masonry and burnt timbers.'

'That was a magnificent stately home,' Oldcastle sighed. 'Your bard, Iolo Goch, said it was a mansion of generosity.'

Owain said, 'I remember that evening in the great hall at Sycharth when Iolo sang a ballad in honour of the Arglwyddes.'

Owain then sang softly as if to himself:

His wife the best of wives!
Happy am I in her wine and mead.
Eminent dame of knightly lineage.
Honourable, beneficent, noble!
Her children come in pairs
A beautiful nest of chieftains.

Opening his eyes, Owain sprang to his feet and shouted in fury, 'My honourable, beneficent, noble Margaret, where is she now? Rotting in a filthy cell waiting for the plague to free her from this wretched life.'

★

Owain, desperate to secure a base for his operations, resolved to attempt the siege of one of the line of castles along the Shropshire border. The decision had not been an easy one as there was the real danger that he would be leading his men to defeat and almost certain carnage. However, through his profound knowledge of history and legend, Owain realised that war was the source of all heroic national myths, and the brightest threads in that glorious tapestry were the lives of leaders who had suffered martyrdom for their cause. By such a death Owain would inspire generations to come.

News of Owain's march towards Shrewsbury reached Henry and he ordered the constable of Welshpool castle to intercept and challenge Owain when he reached the Shropshire border. Owain had sent Henry Don with a small force of cavalry out ahead of the main body of his army.

As dusk fell Don, accompanied by John ap Thomas, reported back to Owain, 'Sire, we observed considerable activity around Welshpool castle that then resolved itself into an army heading in our direction.'

John ap Thomas then said excitedly, 'And, by God, a big army it is too. I'd say at least twice the size of ours.'

Owain asked, 'How was it composed?'

Don answered, 'The vast majority were men-at-arms supplemented by a squadron of cavalry and a body of archers – both of considerable size.'

'You'll need a damned good defensive position when they confront you,' Thomas enjoined. 'But I think Don here has found a solution.'

'I was always taught,' Don averred, 'that when you are heavily outnumbered, shorten your defensive front. Well, about five miles ahead the road is straddled by two dense wooded areas allowing a narrow defile between them of about eight hundred yards. Set up your front line there.'

Owain ordered that they break camp and march forward to this new position. Dawn was breaking when they reached the defile and Owain wasted no time in setting up his defensive position. He chose the narrowest part of the pass and amassed the men-at-arms in the centre with the archers placed on either flank, but slightly forward. This meant that, while his longbow men would have the enemy within arrow-shot, his own men-at-arms would be out of range of the enemy archers. He stationed Henry Don and his cavalry in reserve. When the archers moved into position, they were carrying stout poles sharpened at each end. They forced these into the ground pointing towards the enemy and at an angle that would pierce the chest of a charging horse. Each archer carried a sheaf of twenty-four arrows and before the battle began he would stick these, point down, into the ground at his feet.

At seven o'clock the English army was sighted a mile away and Owain summoned his captains and reminded them that their duty was to stay firm and provoke the enemy into attacking them. He issued an order that each captain was to pass on to his men. 'The English come here to rob us of our independence. It is their part to attack and ours to defend. Count the place where you stand as your hearth-stone. Mark your captains' banners and do not stir from them. To you I give my highest trust. You must not fail. The battle rests with you.'

In a battle, communication is of paramount importance. For the archers to operate effectively, they must receive two orders: the first to draw their bows, the second to fire. Similarly the men-at-arms must know when to advance and when to retreat. These orders were signalled by the raising and lowering of banners and the sounding of horns.

Owain ordered his captains to take up their positions, but asked Alice to remain. When she had abandoned her role as nurse in order to play a full part in the fighting, he had been both excited and repelled by the rapaciousness with which she attacked the enemy. He once again had recurring dreams of a young woman, clothed in golden armour and mounted on a white stallion, riding at the head of a victorious army. He could not decide if this image was relevant to him and his present situation or was a vision of a future event that had nothing to do with him.

Owain stared at the lithe, composed figure standing before him and said, 'Mistress Brut, tell me, why do you fight with the ferocity of a ravening wolf? Why, when you grasp a sword, does your body fill from toe to crown with direst cruelty?'

Alice grimaced and answered, 'Sire, I can assure you my rage is not occasioned by excessive zeal for your cause. I have an intense hatred of the English and their allies. This has its origins in the treatment I received at their hands. Do not question me on that, for it is a subject I will not discuss.'

'Alice, in the battle, I want you to ride with Henry Don's cavalry and wear the armour I have laid out here.'

Owain led Alice over to a table in the corner of the tent and pointed to a golden helmet, cuirass and sword.

Alice cried out, 'But Sire, those are the gifts King Charles sent you in acknowledgement of your prowess as a knight. I cannot wear them.'

Owain persisted, 'You would make an old warrior, who

is possibly fighting his last battle, content if you indulged him in this whim.'

Alice gathered up the armour and walked towards the tent flap, where she turned and said, 'Owain Glyn Dŵr, if we both die in the battle today, it will have been in a noble cause.'

★

Owain, flanked by Maredudd and Madoc, took his place in the centre of the front rank of the men-at-arms. Maredudd, his eyes shining, turned to Owain and exclaimed, 'Father, does this not excite you; this panoply of war – the dissonant blare of the trumpets and the banners streaming in the wind.'

Owain shook his head and said, 'War is but an abhorrent means to achieve a noble purpose. I see no beauty in the slaughter of men.'

This was the moment when Owain fully realised that he had hazarded all on this battle. This field before Shrewsbury was to be as significant for him as the field at Camlann had been for Arthur.

On seeing the disposition of Owain's forces, the constable moved his army to within two hundred and fifty yards of the Welsh line. He placed his cavalry on the left flank and distributed his archers, two ranks deep, as a screen in front of his men-at-arms.

Owain chuckled and said, 'We have him. He should have moved his archers further forward as I have done. Their arrow attack will fall short.'

His eye then fell upon a tall figure with blonde hair riding in front of the enemy lines and exhorting them to battle.

'That figure? It's not the constable,' Owain said.

'No,' Maredudd answered. 'I could swear that knight is Prince Hal. He will make a more formidable adversary than the constable of Welshpool.'

'And make our victory more glorious. All is determined in the mind of God. Signal the longbow men. Let battle commence.'

The red dragon standard was lowered and then raised. The archers drew their bows. The standard was lowered and raised again. The archers released their arrows.

Owain cried out, 'Y Ddraig Goch a ddyry gychwyn.' (The red dragon will show the way.)

He stared up into the sky. The day shone bright and clear, then the sun was obliterated by the dense flight of arrows. The earth and sky reverberated as if with the sound of a thousand hummingbirds. The English archers wore no mail but jerkins of boiled leather and quilted coats, so when the arrows reached their target they reaped a terrible harvest. When Hal attempted to retaliate, the arrows thudded harmlessly into the ground in front of Owain's men-at-arms. Owain ordered his archers to continue their harassment of Hal's men in the hope of inciting them to attack. Provoked beyond endurance, Hal ordered his cavalry to attack Owain's left flank and destroy the archers. Owain watched as Hal led the charge through a hail of arrows and reached the front rank of archers, who then beat an orderly retreat, to reveal the hidden stakes they had driven into the ground. Hal managed to wheel his horse to one side but many reacted too late and were impaled on the vicious, sharpened quills of this monstrous porcupine. Hal, infuriated that he had fallen into such a simple trap, returned to his lines and ordered an advance along the whole front. The archers moved forward stopping at intervals to unleash a volley of arrows, the men-at-arms followed. Owain's men sheltered under their upturned shields and braced themselves for the impact when the two armies met.

In close combat, a foot soldier, armed with a lance, sword,

dagger or battleaxe, would have the ability to kill restricted to a circle of small radius with his body at its centre.

Within minutes of hand-to-hand fighting being joined, many in the front rank of the English had fallen to the ground at the feet of their comrades. This impeded the advance of the whole column. In this situation, the English superiority in numbers was nullified. When Hal, seeing the attack was going nowhere, sounded retreat, Owain signalled to his men to stand firm and not leave their defensive position. Hal launched repeated attacks but the Welsh shield wall remained firm. At noon Hal called a respite and asked permission to remove his dead and wounded from the field. Owain consented and in turn ordered that all his wounded and dead be passed back through the ranks. The men had been so tightly packed, neither slain nor wounded had been able to fall. Owain sensed that Hal was about to make a tactical change and, fearing that his position in the main body of his men was not affording him a full view of the battlefield, he moved, together with Maredudd and Madoc, to an elevation behind his men. Once there, he noted that Hal's cavalry had regrouped and he immediately realised that they were about to charge at the Welsh shield wall. He signalled Don to move his cavalry to the front and meet the challenge of the charging horsemen head-on. Owain watched as Don wheeled his squadron into position and set off at a brisk trot in the direction of the English cavalry. They quickened their pace and soon the two opposing squadrons were charging at full tilt, their banners streaming in their wake. Owain caught his breath as he saw Alice spur her horse past Henry Don and take her place at the head of the charge. His vision of a maid in gold amour riding at the head of his army had become a reality.

When the collision occurred, the slaughter was sickening,

the mangled corpses of men and horses disfigured the ground. Don lay under his horse, pierced through his breastplate by a lance, while near him lay John ap Thomas, his body trampled into the ground. Alice, together with a number of survivors, swept through the enemy and smashed into the oncoming infantry, who turned and ran. The Welsh, elated by the sight of the English in full retreat, ignored Owain's command and streamed from their defensive line in pursuit of the enemy. This situation was purely fortuitous, it was not the result of a ploy by Prince Hal, the flight was genuine. But he now exploited it ruthlessly. He halted the retreat and started a counterattack. Now the fighting was not in a confined space in front of the shield wall but on open ground and it soon developed into a confusion of single combats, where the English superiority in numbers proved irresistible.

Watching in anguish, Owain saw Alice dragged from her horse, stripped of her golden helmet and cuirass and pierced through the heart by a lance. His body trembled and his mouth opened in a silent scream at this swift and brutal shattering of his vision of a triumphant golden maid.

Alarmed, Maredudd spoke urgently, 'The day is lost. You must leave the field.'

He and Madoc hoisted the unresisting Owain onto a horse and the three rode swiftly to the shelter of the nearby wood. When night fell, they were joined by Bishop Trevor Jones and Griffith Young, who reported that three of Owain's most notable captains were now prisoners of Prince Hal.

When Owain asked for their names, Young responded dolefully, 'Rhys the Black, Philip Scudamore of Monmouth and your cousin Rhys ap Tudor.'

'Ah! Rhys,' Owain exclaimed. 'I still chuckle at the way he and his brother outwitted poor John Massy and captured Conway castle.'

Maredudd said bitterly, 'Knowing Hal and his vengeful father, all three heads will end up as barbarous trophies on London Bridge.'

Owain stared into the darkness and appeared to have fallen into a trance. He heard a distant murmur and looked beyond the encircling woods. A host of spectral figures glided towards him: Hotspur, Rhys Gethin, Walter Brut, Rhisiart, John Hanmer, Gruffydd, Henry Don, John ap Thomas, Edmund, three hundred headless figures followed by a host of anonymous warriors. The last was Alice, her golden helmet and cuirass besmirched with blood. In her hand she held a broken sword.

Owain groaned and there burst from his lips an agonised, '*mea culpa.*'

His companions were startled and alarmed by the despair in his voice.

Owain continued, 'Henry Don has led his last cavalry charge; John, my latter-day Wat Tyler, lies silent this night. I beg forgiveness from all the brave men lying dead or dying on the killing field this night, and from all those who have given their lives in previous battles. I pray for the soul of Alice Brut.'

Owain paused and then said wistfully, 'I am a man who has travelled down a road – a road that leads nowhere.'

★

In the weeks and months that followed such a catastrophic defeat, Owain was thrown largely on the defensive, being more concerned with avoiding capture than attacking Henry. However he was still a force to be reckoned with and Henry had to maintain large garrisons at strategic centres in Wales. Such was Owain's reputation among the English that mothers would threaten their disobedient children with a visit from the evil Welsh wizard.

In 1412, his arch enemy David Gam was again captured. A scouting party sent out by Owain surprised a small enemy force encamped near Strata Florida. When the prisoners were brought to Owain's camp, David Gam was discovered among them.

'You have an unfortunate propensity for falling into my hands,' Owain observed. 'Is it some form of death wish?'

Gam answered defiantly, 'Kill me if you wish, but I have had the satisfaction of seeing your downfall. Every castle you held has fallen to Henry and soon your army will be reduced to a pathetic rump. Then you will be hunted like a cur.'

'I still see death close on your heels but I will not be the executioner. You will be ransomed as before and I'm sure your master Henry will, once again, meet my price. You are far too valuable a lapdog to lose.'

Once the ransom was paid, Owain released Gam but he did it with the conviction that Gam would be killed by some other hand on a foreign field. His reluctance to execute Gam was prompted by two considerations: firstly, he needed the ransom money, and secondly Owain still harboured a sense of guilt at the barbaric manner in which he had left broken-backed Hywel Sele, a man whom Gam loved, to die an agonising death in the hollow of a dead oak tree.

Owain and his son fought on as outlaws but, weakened by persistent attacks and the gradual wearing away of moral, the rebel army was reduced to virtual impotence.

CHAPTER 17

Owain meets his grandson John

K ING HENRY LAY asleep in the Jerusalem chamber. It was the cause of muted merriment at court that the King had vowed to make a crusade to the Holy Land and die in Jerusalem, but when he realised that such an undertaking was now beyond his strength, he named his bedchamber Jerusalem, thus achieving part of his vow. On entering the room, Prince Hal saw the crown lying on the pillow beside the King's head. Leaning forward he carefully lifted it up and, turning it around in his hands, gazed in fascination at its golden and bejewelled aspect.

At that instant, Henry woke from a troubled sleep and seeing his son holding the crown said wearily, 'Son, are you so hasty to gain the crown that you mistake my sleep for death?'

'I never thought to hear your speak again.'

'Ah! That thought. Your wish was father to that thought.'

'Never! The seductive brilliance of that golden crown overwhelmed my senses and overlaid my grief, but at no time have I wished your death.'

Henry sighed sadly, 'O foolish youth, you seek a greatness that will engulf you.'

'In my early years I played the fool, as you well know. But, inspired by your example I grew to manhood and fought steadfastly and with much honour at your side against Glendower.'

Hal thrust the crown towards his father with the words, 'Here take the crown, you won it and valiantly have you maintained it. Let God forever keep it from my head.'

'O my son. Come, Hal, sit upon my bed. God knows by what by-paths and crooked ways I gained this crown and I know well how troublesome it sits upon my head. To you it shall descend with better quiet, for all the foulness of my achievement will go with me into the earth, leaving you untainted.'

On March 20th, 1413, Henry IV died peacefully in his sleep and was succeeded by his son. The coronation ceremony was disrupted by a terrible snow storm.

★

Owain Glyn Dŵr had reached the nadir of his fortunes and was in deep despair. After years of desperate campaigning, his captains had been slain or had accepted the King's pardon. Standing outside his tent surrounded by the remnants of his once formidable army, he raised his eyes to the sky and silently prayed, 'O God thy sea is so vast and my frail craft so small.'

A horseman appeared on the distant horizon, riding furiously towards the camp. On reaching Owain, the rider leaped from his horse and knelt at Owain's feet. Owain stared down at the man in consternation and said, 'Please rise, do not mock a man who is so acquainted with grief.'

Maredudd rose and gathering Owain in his arms, said, 'Father, do you not know your own son?'

'A son who deserts his father and accepts the King's pardon,' Owain said bitterly.

'I come from Hal to offer you and the others a similar pardon. Now that he is King, Hal has had King Richard's body disinterred from its obscure grave and brought to the

Abbey where Richard now lies among his fellow kings. By such gestures Hal wishes to reconcile the peoples of this island and reign in peace.'

'It is more likely that he wants this land pacified so that he can pursue his ambitions in France.'

'Father, look around you. You no longer present a challenge to the English throne. Where are the men of substance who once supported you?'

'Dead or deserters,' Owain said sadly. But then he stared defiantly at Maredudd and added, 'All but my chancellor Griffith Young, who is still active in my cause at the French court, and has been made Bishop of Bangor by Benedict XIII.'

Realising that further argument would be fruitless, Maredudd tried a fresh approach, 'While you wait for French assistance, you will need a sanctuary and I have just the place.'

'Where?'

'Your daughter's house in Herefordshire.'

'John Scudamore's house?'

Maredudd nodded.

'You must be mad,' Owain said.

'No! I have spoken to Alys and her husband. They would welcome you into their home and have assured me that the secluded nature of the property would ensure your security.'

'But why are they willing to take such a risk?'

'Alys told me that when she rode away from Glyndyfrdwy that fateful day, you and she exchanged a look of deep affection. Over the years her feelings have not changed. As for her husband, he has held you in high regard ever since he fought against you at Carreg Cennen. Also remember that his cousin Philip was one of your finest captains. The Scudamore family have always been ambivalent in their loyalties.'

Owain reluctantly agreed to take refuge in his daughter's home at Monnington Straddel, Golden Valley in Herefordshire.

★

Three horsemen, heavily cloaked and hooded, rode through the screening forest and dismounted before the entrance to Monnington Straddel. Maredudd knocked on the oak door and when it opened the three men entered the house. There in the hall they were greeted by a man of military bearing, his sleek black hair streaked with grey.

Maredudd spoke first, 'Sir John Scudamore, may I introduce my father Owain Glyn Dŵr and his servant Madoc.'

Madoc muttered under his breath, 'I would prefer bodyguard and friend.'

Scudamore stepped forward and addressing Owain, said, 'Father-in-law, I welcome you to my house.'

Owain nodded his head and said, 'I admired your defence at Carreg Cennen and vowed I would shake your hand if ever we met.'

Owain grasped John's hand and shook it vigorously. He added, 'You will only be burdened with my presence. Madoc will depart with my son, having, like him, made his peace with the English crown.'

'It was not my wish,' Madoc protested gruffly.

Owain laid his hand on Madoc's shoulder and said gently, 'Believe me old friend, it is for the best.'

Mollified by Owain's reference to him as an old friend, Madoc said, 'How I wish I could stay with you until your dying day. But I bow to your authority and will depart with Maredudd. But it will be with a heart burdened by sorrow.'

Maredudd, in the grip of two conflicting emotions – relief that his father was now in a safe house, exasperation that he refused to accept the King's pardon – said briskly, 'Come Madoc, it's time we departed.'

Their departure was swift, leaving Scudamore and Owain staring at the heavy door as it slowly swung shut.

Scudamore was the first to speak, 'Sire, come, your daughter and grandson await you in the great hall.'

When Owain entered the room, Alys was on her knees playing with a young boy. The stone floor was covered with small wooden soldiers laid out in an intricate pattern. The boy glanced at Owain and then turned his attention back to his soldiers. Alys rose to her feet and walked slowly towards Owain. She had not altered over the years and Owain felt transposed to that day when she rode out of his life. They embraced in silence, there being no words capable of expressing their feelings.

Scudamore, who had been watching the scene from the open doorway, called, 'John! Come and say hello to your grandfather. He is a great and famous knight.'

John sprang to his feet and, running up to Owain, said confidently, 'I know everything about knights. I'm an expert on the subject.'

Owain, noting the auburn hair and blue eyes, acknowledged the boy's English ancestry, but was pleased to see his Welsh origins manifested in his short, sturdy figure.

Owain asked, 'What battle is taking place over there?'

'King Richard, the Lionheart, leading the Crusaders against Saladin's infidels.'

'And the battle?'

Without a moment's hesitation, John answered, 'The famous victory won by Richard at Arsuf during the Third Crusade. Richard's army was under heavy attack from

Saladin's Muslims. Richard forbade his men to counterattack until the evening when he launched a general charge that swept all before him.'

At that moment, Owain realised that he could find sanctuary and contentment here at Monnington Straddel with Alys and his grandson John.

★

Owain had the instinct of a teacher, the desire to pass on information – to enlighten all he met. Madoc had been the target of this obsession during their days in the wilderness but now, that his daughter had re-entered his life, he seized the opportunity to acquaint her with the history of her family.

Finding her alone, embroidering a tapestry that appeared to be, by the abundance of flora and fauna, a representation of the tree of life, he sat beside her and spoke, 'My child, I know that your situation here has forced you to conceal your provenance, but you should carry in your heart the knowledge of your noble ancestry.'

Alys, somewhat discomforted by her father's pompous manner, looked up, startled.

Owain continued, 'My child you are of aristocratic stock, directly descended from the Princes of Powys and Cyfeiliog. I am, on my father's side a member of the dynasty of northern Powys and on my mother's side descended from that of Deheubarth in the south.'

Alys gathered up her courage and asked this white-bearded, defeated old man, 'Father, I have, in my own casual way studied the history of Wales. Tell me why Wales has found it so difficult to become a united, independent nation?'

Pleased by the acuity of Alys' question, Owain replied, 'The Welsh inheritance laws.'

Seeing Alys' puzzled look, Owain said, 'In England lands and titles are passed on to the eldest son, under the primogeniture law. But in Wales everything is divided between competing heirs. This situation prevents the emergence of a single dominant leader. The first lord to defy this rule was Llywelyn ap Iorwerth, some now refer to him as Llewelyn the Great. Born in 1178 he was the grandson of Owain Gwynedd, prince of Gwynedd. When he died, the estate was divided between Llywelyn and his two uncles.'

'What about Llywelyn's father? Wasn't he a competing heir?'

'He was disabled in some way, and as a result was considered unsuitable. His nickname, Flat Face, suggests a facial disfigurement. Llywelyn rose up against his uncles and defeated them to become the sole ruler of Gwynedd. He extended his power base into the south and became the most powerful figure in Wales. Llywelyn had three sons – Gruffydd, Dafydd and Tegwared – and he knew that, by law, when he died his estate would have to be divided between the three. To keep his domain intact, he declared Dafydd his sole heir and gained the support of the Pope and Henry III. He summoned all the petty princes of Wales to the Cistercian abbey of Strata Florida and made them swear allegiance to Dafydd. This all proved in vain when he died in 1240. Although the most powerful leader in Wales, the English crown had never officially recognised him as Prince of Wales and once he was dead other Welsh claimants reneged on their promises.'

'What happened then?'

Owain shook his head and said, 'Chaos, and then Llywelyn ap Gruffydd. But that's enough for today.'

During these early weeks at Monnington Straddle, Owain grew very fond of his seven-year-old grandson, whom he found to be mature beyond his tender years. Owain delighted in engaging the lad in conversation. He believed in increasing the boy's vocabulary by using difficult words, a ploy he had never used with Madoc.

★

The family had an old hunting dog named Gyp and when the dog died, Owain thought he would comfort John by telling him the story of Gelert, Llywelyn the Great's faithful hound. For some reason he thought this tragic story would comfort the lad.

'The great prince had a palace at Beddgelert and on the occasions when he sojourned there he would often go out hunting with his faithful hound Gelert. One morning Gelert did not go hunting with Llywelyn.'

'Excuse me, excuse me,' interrupted John. 'Why did Gelert not go hunting with Llywelyn?'

'Well, I don't really know. Anyway, it doesn't matter why Gelert stayed in the palace. The relevant point is that he did stay in the palace. When Llywelyn returned from the hunt, Gelert joyfully sprang to welcome his master. Llywelyn was alarmed when he saw Gelert covered in blood, and he hastened to the palace where he found his infant son's cot empty and the bedclothes smeared with blood. He immediately assumed that Gelert had killed the boy and plunged his sword into the poor hound's side. Gelert's dying yelp was followed by a child's cry. When Llywelyn made a thorough search of the room he found his son alive. The body of a mighty wolf, slain by Gelert, lay at the child's side. Llywelyn was filled with remorse for he had killed the faithful hound who had saved his son and heir.'

'He should have made a more careful search that first time,'

John said coolly. 'Don't worry about my reaction to Gyp's, death. I will be sad but will remember all the happy times I had with Gyp. It will be the same when you die, Grandfather. I will be sad but then I will remember the happy times we had together and I will be content.'

John looked up at Owain and asked, 'Grandfather, why do I find stories so important?'

'Stories are important to us all, to people of different times and cultures. They entertain us but, more importantly, they remind us of the past and of our cultural identity.'

'What is cultural identity?'

'It is what defines the character of a nation. Your cultural identity is to be found in the history of the Kings of Britain and the tales recounted in the *Red Book of Hergest* and the *White Book of Rhydderch*. Some stories have a universal significance as they speak of man's relationship to God, or the Gods, depending on your religious beliefs.'

'What tales are these?'

'The Old and New Testaments and the Bhagavad-Gita attempt to explain the nature of man's presence in the universe.'

'Could you, Grandfather, make up a story?'

Owain was taken aback but said, 'I'll tell you a tale about life and death. The two topics we were speaking about earlier. In the far distant past in a land on the other side of the world there lived a very remarkable king.'

'What was his name?'

Owain hesitated for an instant then said, 'King Gilgamesh and his kingdom was the city of Uruk.'

John interrupted, 'How can a city be a kingdom?'

'O my boy, in those ancient times, city states were the order of the day. Now to continue, Gilgamesh had a divine mother and a human father. Being half-human and half-divine, his courage, energy and strength were so great that the demands he made on his people, who were just ordinary mortals, wore them out. They became so desperate that they appealed to the gods to help them. The gods created Enkidu to be a companion for the King. They fashioned him from clay and hair. Then, having had him reared by wild animals in the jungle, they presented him to the King. The pair complemented each other, one being half-divine and half-human the other being half-divine and half-animal. They went around the world performing heroic deeds and the King's people were left in peace. However the gods, watching these strapping, resplendent men slaying dragons and rescuing maidens, became jealous and struck down Enkidu with a mortal sickness. Gilgamesh held his dying friend in his arms until he felt the life drain from Enkidu's body. Gazing down on the corpse of his beloved friend, the King made a vow that he would conquer death. Setting aside his royal robes and his golden crown, Gilgamesh travelled to the end of the world and, after passing through the Garden of the Gods, where all the trees were hung with multicoloured jewels of great beauty, he reached the Sea of Death. Desperate to find the secret of immortality, he set sail across its black, turbulent waters. Imagine his surprise when, in the middle of this desolate ocean, he discovered an island whose only inhabitants were an ancient couple. The venerable old man informed Gilgamesh that his name was Noe and that the Gods had granted him and his wife immortality and placed them on this inaccessible island, where they were destined to live for all of eternity. Greatly excited by this news, Gilgamesh asked why the Gods had conferred this boon on Noe and his wife. Noe explained that, many hundreds of years ago, the Gods had decided to wipe out all human and animal life by means of a devastating flood. One of the Gods was not happy with this and helped

Noe build a boat large enough to house, and so save, male and female pairs of all the worlds species of animals and humans. After the flood, the Gods regretted what they had done and were so delighted with Noe's action that they granted him and his wife immortality. Gilgamesh then demanded that Noe tell him how he, Gilgamesh, could make the gods confer immortality on him. Noe smiled sadly and said that there was no way the gods would assign to any other human being the gift of eternal life. He did, however, give Gilgamesh a magic plant and told him that, though it would not make him immortal, it would renew his youth. Every time he ate of its fruit he would become young again, just as a snake sheds its old skin. But, like the snake, he would eventually die. Noe warned Gilgamesh of the horrors he would meet if he continued his voyage across the Sea of Death, and persuaded him to return home. On the journey back to Uruk, Gilgamesh zealously guarded the plant but one night, as he slept, a snake entered his tent and devoured the precious object. So Gilgamesh returned to Uruk as empty-handed as when he had left it. He had, however, learnt that death was the fate of all human beings, irrespective of fortune or fame.'

John said with satisfaction, 'It's as I said, one must be content.'

Owain laughed and said, 'So you did, my boy. So you did.'

'Grandfather, that character Noe seems very like Noah to me.'

'Every civilisation has its ark.'

★

A little while later, his grandson revealed another side of his nature. Owain had been relating how Vortigern had been burnt to death in his supposedly impregnable castle.

The boy appeared upset and said curtly, 'Impossible! How can stones burn?'

Owain answered, 'Believe me, John, an awful lot of wood goes into the construction of a castle.'

John reluctantly accepted Owain's explanation but it was obvious that he was disturbed. Owain thought it strange that a lad who would listen to tales of bloody battles and the severing of heads with equanimity could be so upset by the idea of a man burning to death. Owain looked more keenly at John and noticed the fear in his eyes. The fact that a man could burn to death in a castle that he had been assured was impregnable, made the boy aware of the danger that lurked in the world.

'I love you Grandfather,' John said. 'If anything goes wrong here, you'll look after me, won't you?'

Owain grasped John's hand and said, 'On the word of a prince.'

★

Like any young child, John was constantly asking questions, though the nature of his questions might be regarded as being more than a little esoteric for a seven year old.

'Grandfather, tell me all about the bards and how they made human sacrifices.'

Owain looked puzzled and said, 'Bards making human sacrifices? No, no, boy, you are mistaken. Bards are, for the most part, gentle poets. They are the remembrancers to a dynasty and its people. They don't go round sacrificing human beings.'

'Yes they did, Grandfather,' John cried impatiently. 'And they all lived on the island of Anglesey until the Romans came and killed them.'

Owain's face cleared and he said, laughingly, 'Those were Druids not bards. In the distant past, the Druids were the priests of the Celtic tribes. They wielded great power and in council had the right to speak before the King. They acted as ambassadors at time of war and were the force that held together Celtic culture.'

'And they practised human sacrifice,' persisted John.

'Yes, you bloodthirsty little monster, and animal sacrifice too. All we know of them now we owe to the written records left by the Romans. But we must remember that it suited the Romans to portray the Druids as barbarians and the Romans as a great civilising force. In AD 61 the Romans exterminated the Druids of Anglesey. Tacitus gives us an account of the battle in his *Annals*. The opposing army with its dense array of fierce warriors stood on the opposite shore, while between the ranks dashed women in black attire like the Furies of Greek myth with their painted faces suffused with malice, their wild silver hair flying in the wind, their clawing fingers tipped with long cruel nails. All around the Druids lifted up their hands to the heavens and poured forth dreadful curses. The Romans, inspired by their general's exhortations, bore their standards forward and smote down all resistance.'

'Was that the end of the Druids?'

'It certainly was, my boy.'

'Why were the Romans so mighty?'

'In the ancient world, there was no civilisation more powerful than Rome. Its governance took the form of an absolute monarchy. The Emperor exercised total power over its citizens. He commanded the army, and all executive, judicial and legislative procedures were in his hands. The Roman Empire extended from the Bay of Biscay in the west to the river Euphrates in the east and from the borders of Scotland in the north to the Sahara in the south. Wherever the emperor went, the army marched with him. Behind the serried ranks of disciplined soldiers, came the tax-collectors and lawyers, the functionaries of the Roman bureaucracy. The regime did not allow any form of self-government in its occupied territories, as it feared such institutions would encourage political dissent.'

★

Owain soon settled into a routine at Monnington Straddel. During the day, he took over the role of his grandson's companion and tutor. The child asked Owain how knowledge and understanding progressed from age to age.

Owain responded, 'The history of intellectual development can be likened to a relay race. An enterprising culture picks up a torch, runs as far as it can and hands it on to a younger civilisation before falling exhausted to the ground. The ancient Greeks ignited the flame of intellectual enquiry and passed it on to the Romans. The Barbarians invaded Rome and extinguished the flame. However the flame still flickered in the empire of Byzantium and when the Arabs stormed Europe they not only brought death and destruction, but algebra and the glory that was Greece. A neat analogy but not, I'm afraid, completely satisfactory.'

'In what way?'

'Different cultures overlap each other. The bards of our time perform the same services as the ancient Greek poets – they are the romancers of history.'

Owain and John played war games on the polished surface of the dining room table, Owain's ageing limbs preventing him squatting on the cold flagstones.

Sir Lancelot rescued Queen Guinevere from the stake; King Arthur and his knights routed the army of the treacherous

Mordred; King Alfred defeated the fierce Vikings; King Richard, the Lionheart, led the Crusaders across the burning sands of Palestine to meet the Saracen hordes of the chivalrous Emir Saladin.

Owain and John would explore the grounds and environs of the house, while Owain, with an eloquence worthy of Iolo Goch, told his grandson of a time before King Arthur, an age populated by mighty warriors – Cassivellaunus, Caractacus, Constantine, Constans, Aurelius Ambrosius, Uther Pendragon, Hengist, Horsa and the traitor Vortigern.

When John asked what happened after Arthur, Owain sighed and answered, 'The number and intensity of Anglo-Saxon invasions increased until the Britons were pushed back to the Celtic fringes and an Anglo-Saxon England emerged from the smouldering wreckage of Britain. It was an England that endured for over 500 years until, in 1066, Duke William of Normandy defeated King Harold of England at the Battle of Hastings.'

'What effect did this have on England?'

'Considerable, my boy. The Anglo-Saxon ruling class was replaced by a Norman-French elite. A nation in which the rulers spoke the same language as the ruled became, overnight, a state that was administered in Latin and governed in French.'

'That isn't how I now see England.'

'No and I'll tell you why. Forty years after the Battle of Hastings, the institutions and values of the old Anglo-Saxon state still survived and came to dominate medieval England.'

John looked puzzled. 'How was that?' he asked.

'We find many instances in history where a nation that militarily defeats another, is itself culturally conquered by the nation it defeated. It happened when Rome militarily conquered the Greeks but, because the Greeks were far more civilised than the Romans, Rome embraced Greek culture. The Roman poet Virgil based his great poem *Aeneid* on Homer's *Odyssey* and *Iliad*.'

'Was William a greater warrior than Harold? After all he did win the battle.'

'You must remember that before the battle Harold had raced north to Stamford Bridge and defeated the combined forces of Hardrada, the King of Norway, and Tostig, Harold's rebellious brother. Then came news that William had landed in Pevensey. Harold was forced to march his battle-weary soldiers back south to face William at Hastings.

'The night before the battle, the English spent their time drinking and singing. The Normans passed the night confessing their sins and in the morning received holy communion.

'On foot, armed with battle-axes and protected by their shields, the English took their stand on the brow of a hill and formed an impenetrable shield wall. Harold, surrounded by his housecarls, took up his position beside his standard, which bore the figure of a warrior woven with the purest gold thread. His housecarls were of towering stature, their gilded mail, inlaid axes and gold-hilted swords glinted in the early morning sunshine.

'The Norman infantry, armed with bows and arrows, formed the vanguard while the cavalry, divided into two wings was placed in the rear.

'A supremely confident William declared that his side was the righteous side and that God would favour them.

'Harold's exhortation to his warriors was far more prosaic. He ordered them to stand firm and not let the enemy break the shield wall and he counselled them that the enemy would feign flight and try to draw them down but they must not leave their station.

'William launched repeated assaults up the hill but all

were met with resolute resistance and the English defences remained intact throughout the day. Then William resorted to the tactic Harold had foretold, he ordered his men to feign retreat. Believing that the victory was theirs, the English streamed down the slope and were destroyed by William's cavalry. This left just Harold and his housecarls holding the top of the hill. Their resistance was truly heroic, as with axe and sword they struck down the enemy, felling a knight and his horse with one blow. Harold was slain when an arrow pierced his eye, he died still grasping his Golden Warrior standard. His housecarls formed a protective ring round his prostrate body and fought to the last man. When Harold's body was brought to William he washed and anointed it with his own hands. At dawn, Harold was buried in unhallowed ground on the high cliffs above the port of Hastings. On the gravestone were engraved the words:

A King, Harold, by a Duke's will you rest here,
Still guardian of the shore and of the sea.

'I feel rather sorry for Harold, now that I know the whole story,' John said sadly. 'But who had right on his side and who was the greater warrior?'

'To answer your first question, on his death bed William is reported to have said: "By wrong I conquered England. By wrong I seized the kingdom to which I have no right."'

'So that answers that. The second question is not so straightforward. Harold and William were well matched. There were not two such warriors beneath the sun. I'd liken them to Hector and Achilles.'

'I'll choose Harold,' John said emphatically. 'For me he is, like his banner, a Golden Warrior.'

'You have chosen well. There was always a streak of

sadistic ruthlessness in William. To achieve his objective, he would often put out the eyes of a hostage or prisoner in full view of the victim's compatriots.'

'Tell me, Grandfather, how do you know so much about the past?'

'During the reign of Alfred, a group of monks began the process of recording and bringing to life a thousand years of England's history – from the birth of Christ to the coronation of King Henry II. This record, beautifully illuminated by numerous illustrations and decorative page borders, we know as *The Anglo-Saxon Chronicles*. We are also indebted to such scholars and historians, as the Venerable Bede, William of Malmesbury and Geoffrey of Monmouth.'

On occasions, Owain spoke movingly of the people who had played major roles in his life – the Arglwyddes, Gruffydd, Maredudd, Catherine, Rhisiart, Rhys Gethin, Griffith Young, Walter Brut and others. There was one about whom he kept silent, Alice Brut. He had never understood the emotions she had evoked in his breast.

When John asked him about King Richard, Owain replied sadly, 'Many believed him to be a vain and vacillating king who lavished gifts and preferment on a handful of sycophantic favourites. But I will always remember that at the age of fourteen, while Bolingbroke cowered for safety in the Tower, he rode out to Smithfield and pacified the rebellious mob that was ravaging London. Now that was the action of a truly great king.'

At night, with John safely in bed, Owain would converse with Alys and his son-in-law in their elegant drawing room. Although still placing his faith in Griffith Young, Owain was beginning to slip into a reluctant acceptance of the hopelessness of his situation.

CHAPTER 18

A burial at Monnington Straddel

THE ROMAN CATHOLIC Church was riven by the rivalry between the Pope at Rome and the Pope at Avignon. In 1409 an ecumenical council was called at Pisa. It deposed the two existing popes and appointed a third. The trouble was that the two deposed popes refused to co-operate, with the farcical result that Christendom now had three popes, thus worsening the schism. In 1414 another council was called at Constance. Its primary aim was to reunite the church but also to examine and pronounce on the writings of John Wycliffe and Jan Hus.

Owain's chancellor, Griffith Young, was still in France assiduously promoting his master's cause. It should, therefore, be no surprise to find, when the council opened, Young sitting among the French delegates.

A representative from the English delegation rose and made a proposal. 'I humbly submit that in this council, voting should not be by dioceses but by nations.'

Prompted by Griffith, a French delegate intervened, 'I object to the inclusion of the Welsh within this English nation. The Welsh are not part of the English nation, they are themselves a nation – the Welsh nation.'

While this was not a military victory, it was a psychological one. News of Griffith's continued presence in France kept alive Owain's hope of ultimate victory against all the odds.

The council elected as the legitimate Pope, Oddone

Colonna, who became Martin V, and thus ended the schism. The writings of John Wycliffe and Jan Hus were condemned as heretical. Wycliffe, having died twenty years earlier, was beyond their barbaric punishment but poor Hus was burnt at the stake.

★

One evening Alys was working intently on her tree of life, a canvas that appeared to have the capacity for infinite expansion, while Owain and Scudamore were discussing Welsh affairs in general, and previous Welsh princes in particular.

'I would be interested to learn your views on Llywelyn ap Iorwerth, the one with the sobriquet Great,' Scudamore said.

'He brought Wales under his control but acted more as the head of a federation of principalities than an absolute monarch. He did, however, punish any opposition to his will with ruthless force.'

'Yes Owain, but, at any given time, Llywelyn's authority and power depended on the attitude and policies of whoever sat on the English throne.'

'I'm afraid what you say is true. While Llywelyn behaved as a dependent prince and posed no threat to England, he was tolerated. In 1205, Llywelyn took Joan, the illegitimate daughter of King John, as his wife but six years later King John, a weak and vacillating ruler, turned against Llywelyn and, marching into north-east Wales, inflicted a devastating defeat on the Welsh that brought Llywelyn to his knees. This caused the Welsh to rise up and unite behind Llywelyn. It was then that he demonstrated his strategical and tactical skills. Exploiting the strife between John and his barons, Llywelyn was, over a period of 28 years, able to restore the territories he had lost and to establish once again his authority over Wales.

Llywelyn's reign was a golden age for Wales. He refined Wales' laws, built castles and encouraged its artists and bards. Near the end of his life Llywelyn suffered a stroke and retired to Aberconwy Abbey where he died in 1240. Tragically, that golden age did not survive his death.'

Scudamore said, with a short laugh, 'Well he showed that you didn't have to die a martyr or become a myth to successfully fight for Welsh independence.'

Owain sighed and said, 'Unlike poor Gruffudd ap Llywelyn, putative Prince of Wales when Edward the Confessor ruled England.'

'What of him?'

'His defeat in 1063 provoked an uprising against him and, like Darius, he was slain by his own men, who sent his severed head to Edward as a trophy.'

Owain paused and then continued, 'But returning to Llywelyn ap Iorwerth, the English never officially recognised Llywelyn as Prince of Wales. His power rested on his own personality and political luck. Neither of which survived his death. He came closer than any other to realising the ambition of creating an independent Wales. If Llywelyn ap Iorwerth failed, there is little hope that any other will succeed.

'What I don't understand is that having left such a firm foundation for an independent Wales, it all came to nothing and you count Llywelyn ap Iorwerth a failure.'

Alys looked up from her tapestry and said, 'The Welsh system of inheritance, raised its ugly head yet again. Llywelyn had three sons – Gruffydd, Dafydd and Tegwared – and he knew that when he died his estate would have to be divided between his three sons. To prevent this, he declared Dafydd his sole heir and made all the petty princes swear allegiance to Dafydd. This was all in vain and once he died other claimants reneged on their promises.'

'You seem very knowledgeable,' Scudamore remarked.

Alys laughed and said, 'Father told me all about it earlier.'

Owain nodded his head and said, 'To continue this tale of woe, Dafydd, in an attempt to be Llywelyn's undisputed heir, held his brothers in captivity and then handed them over to Henry III who promptly placed them in the Tower of London. Gruffydd, in attempting to escape, fell to his death from his cell at the top of the Tower. Relations between King Henry and Dafydd deteriorated and war broke out. This is the point when Llywelyn ap Gruffydd makes his appearance. He was the second of Gruffydd's four sons and he boldly entered the fray on Dafydd's side.'

Scudamore interjected, 'You are speaking here of Llywelyn the Last?'

'Yes, Llywelyn Ein Llyw Olaf, the grandson of Llywelyn the Great. When Dafydd died, Llywelyn by force of arms asserted his right to be Prince of Wales. Taking advantage of the dispute between King Henry III and the barons, Llywelyn allied himself with Simon de Montfort, Henry's chief opponent. When Simon de Montfort was slain in 1265, Llywelyn signed a treaty in which he was authorised to receive the homage of the other Welsh princes in return for recognising the overlordship of the English king. On Henry's death and the accession of Edward I, Llywelyn rebelled again only to be defeated by Edward. Llywelyn was nothing if not persistent and in 1282 he and his brother David rose again to fight for independence. The rising was crushed when Edward's forces killed Llywelyn in a battle near Brecon.'

'How would you sum up his achievements?'

'On the credit side, he was the only Welsh leader to be officially recognised by the English as Prince of Wales. On the debit side, within a year of his death, Wales lay crushed beneath a brutal English heel.'

'Well,' Alys said, 'Llywelyn the Great has my vote. He ruled Wales for 28 years and laid the foundations for a permanent independent Wales. It was not his fault that later generations dissipated his legacy.'

Owain, as if speaking his thoughts aloud, said, 'My rebellion is not an attempt to restore the old Wales of mythical history and the laws of Hywel. Those had faded into oblivion before the start of my rebellion. I am not an archaic leader making a stand for an old Wales but a visionary attempting to create a new Wales that can take its place among the modern nations of the world.'

Alys carefully folded her tapestry, laid it to one side and said, 'It's late and I'm off to bed.'

Both men rose, bowed and then resumed their seats and their conversation.

Scudamore, changing the topic, asked, 'Was Arthur an archaic leader?'

'By archaic do you mean that Arthur has no relevance for us today?'

'That's exactly what I mean.'

'We first meet Arthur in the poems of ancient Welsh bards.'

Owain declaimed:

And then Arthur gathered together
all the men that were in
the three islands of Britain.
And he went with all those men to Ireland.
And there was great fear and
shaking because of him.
And when Arthur landed,
all the saints of Ireland
came to him to beg for mercy.

For a moment, Owain paused and then said with a sigh, 'Geoffrey of Monmouth took this shadowy figure from Welsh legend and created a Normanesque hero. According to Geoffrey of Monmouth, Arthur was a king who united Britain under his rule and then invaded Europe. When he reached the gates of Rome he received news that his nephew Mordred had abducted the queen and claimed the throne. Arthur returned and fought Mordred at the battle of Camlann, where both were slain.'

Scudamore said eagerly, 'In the Arthurian saga, we see depicted: chivalry, courtesy, virtue, humanity, friendship, love, bravery, cowardice, murder, hate and sin.'

Owain smiled indulgently and said, 'The tales of knightly chivalry, Lancelot's love for Guinevere, the idea that Mordred was Arthur's son begot incestuously upon Arthur's sister, are all embellishments added at a later date by French writers, the chief of whom was Chrétien de Troyes. Arthur was honoured by his contemporaries, and men who came after him, as a great warrior who for many years reigned over a land where rulers, public persons and private, bishops and clergy, each kept their proper station.'

'Good stable government, then?'

'Yes, where the parameters of truth and justice were observed.'

'Some confusion regarding his ancestry, though.'

Owain shook his head and said, 'His name suggests his origin. Artorius is a common Roman name. Since Arthur's death a wealth of myth and legend, much of it enshrined in Geoffrey of Monmouth's *History of the Kings of Britain,* has replaced the rather prosaic truth of Arthur's life and exploits. He might well have been nothing more than the leader of a war-band holding at bay the invading Saxons.'

'Why did Geoffrey write this book?'

'At that time there was no definitive account of British history and he took the chance to exhort the Welsh to remember their glorious past. He also hoped to ingratiate himself with the Normans who ruled Britain. As we look back at the age of Arthur, our vision is obscured by this image of a gigantic mythical warrior created by the versifiers of France and the bards of Wales.'

Scudamore leant forward and said, 'Owain Glyn Dŵr. How will history look back on you?'

Owain stared into the glowing embers of the dying fire and said nothing.

★

The establishment at Monnington Straddel was a modest one consisting of two maids and a groom. They were fully aware of who Owain was but kept the secret out of a sense of loyalty and the fact that they had grown fond of the old man. Scudamore was so afraid of betrayal that he ordered his groom to keep a horse saddled day and night ready for swift flight. Although Owain's place of sanctuary was widely known among his supporters, no one betrayed him.

Early in September 1415, Maredudd and Madoc visited Owain with unwelcome news. They were shocked by the change in Owain's appearance, instead of the vigorous, keen-eyed, combative prince they had brought to Monnington, they were confronted by man whose voice and gestures exhibited the symptoms of advancing years.

'Son, what news from France,' Owain enquired eagerly.

Maredudd cast a worried glance at Madoc, before replying, 'Not good, I'm afraid. Chancellor Young is so disappointed with the progress he is making in France that he is contemplating making his way to Rome and ask forgiveness at the feet of the Pope.'

'In the hope that the Pope will provide him with a bishopric,' Madoc said sarcastically.

Owain responded sharply, 'No Madoc, you are wrong. Griffith is a splendid and remarkable fellow, who has served me loyally.'

Maredudd said, 'Father, I believe he is already on his way to Rome.'

Owain's face went white as the blood flowed from his cheeks.

Maredudd continued remorselessly, 'King Henry is preparing a force to invade France and many of your fearsome longbow men and men-at-arms are joining his army as mercenaries.'

'And you, son,' Owain asked, 'What are you going to do?'

'Join them. What else am I trained to do? Madoc and I will be a part of that expeditionary force. Face it father, your rebellion is over. Accept the pardon that Henry offers.'

Owain drew himself upright and said with great dignity, 'Never! Never will Owain Glyn Dŵr bend his knee to an English king.'

'Llywelyn ap Gruffydd did.'

'Yes and look what happened. Slain on the battlefield and his nation in chains.'

Before they left, a form of reconciliation was made between Owain and his son. Madoc broke down completely and declared that he would stay by Owain's side for the rest of his life.

Owain answered gently, 'Madoc, your future lies fighting at the side of my son not dancing attendance on a defeated, ailing, old man. Serve him as you have served me and I will be comforted.'

To his son, he gave his blessing, 'Your decision grieves

me, but you are of my flesh and blood and my blessing must go with you. For what an unnatural father I would be to curse my son. Heed my words, to your own self be true and it will follow that you will not be false to any man. If King Henry is now your liege lord, serve him loyally with diligence and honour. I would have it no other way.'

★

That night Owain lay on his bed with his eyes staring into the darkness and prayed for the liberating light of day. There came flooding into his mind the shocking sight of the obscenely mutilated bodies of the English lying on the slopes of Bryn Glas.

In the morning, finding he could not summon the energy to rise, he called for Alys and asked her to sit beside him.

Taking her hand, he said, 'Last night I took a journey back in time when these islands were inhabited by a primitive people. They were divided into warlike tribes, each with its own petty king. They believed in two major gods, the male great god and the female great god. He was a grotesque figure who carried a massive club with which he inflicted mighty blows on his victims, though sometimes he would reward them with gifts from his huge cauldron of rebirth. She displayed the attributes of fertility and destructiveness, and seemed to turn from a fertile woman to hideous hag at will. These two gods worked in unison with the tribal kings. When a king's power waned, they presided over his ritual execution. The whole ethos of this society was based on blood sacrifice. The victims were not only expendable kings, everyone was in danger of being sacrificed – prisoners, women and babies. In every village there were the instruments of execution and the smell of blood.

'I first met the concept of a cauldron of rebirth in the folktale, 'Branwen Daughter of Llŷr', in the form of a giant pot, which had the property that if the mutilated body of a slain warrior was cast into its black interior, he would emerge the next day alive and whole but without the power of speech. It is a story of senseless slaughter and horror – a young boy is thrust head first into a raging fire. Why is our folklore so obsessed with blood and terror? What does that tell us about our ancestors? Are we as a nation about to slip back into such barbarity?'

Alys stroked his hand in an effort to comfort him.

Owain continued, 'I dreamt of a Welsh church free of Canterbury, with its own metropolitan at St Davids. A church where Welsh clerics spoke their native language and the revenues were devoted to Welsh needs. I dreamt of a parliament whose members were tribunes of the people. I dreamt of two universities, one in the north, the other in the south. But most of all, I dreamt of a nation at peace with itself, where its citizens lived under a just judiciary and equitable laws.'

Owain paused and then said bitterly, 'With such ancestors, how could I have hoped to fulfil such a dream?'

Alys protested, 'But we are not like those barbarians, the years of Roman occupation civilised our people.'

'Straight roads and central heating cannot destroy the atavistic nature of a people; it can only disguise it.'

★

It took a week before Owain Glyn Dŵr relinquished his hold on life. He spent this time semi-conscious on his bed with his grandson faithfully keeping vigil. It was certainly not the heroic death that a great warrior and statesman might have expected. The instant the death rattle sounded in his throat, a large tear rolled slowly down his cheek — a bitter tear, for Owain had died with his sacred task unfulfilled.

There came into Alys' mind an old saying, 'The sorrow is deep when dead men weep.'

They buried Owain in a secluded part of the garden and no cross was left to mark the spot. This was done not out of indifference but out of a desire to protect the sanctity of his corpse.

As the small burial party walked away, his grandson tried hard to remember the happy times they had spent together but it afforded him no comfort and he was not content.

Alys said, 'Owain was not of the common order. He may have died an embittered man but he will live on in the hearts of all Welshmen.'

Epilogue

IN OCTOBER 1415, Henry V was returning from an abortive attempt to seize the French throne. His army was depleted by casualties and disease and when he reached the castle at Agincourt he found the road to Calais blocked by a French army of vastly superior numbers. Henry realised that his only hope of survival was to goad the French into making a full-frontal assault. For the past week there had been torrential downpours and the ground was sodden. This should have slowed down the heavily armoured knights, giving his longbow men the opportunity to create havoc among their ranks. By advancing his first line of men-at-arms, he succeeded in provoking the arrogant French knights to charge the English line. As Henry had foreseen, the French became trapped in the muddy ground and were cut down by the English archers. Three times the French mounted a cavalry charge and three times they were repulsed with horrendous casualties. Sensing that the time had come to apply the *coup de grâce*, Henry led a charge of a few hundred knights at the demoralised foe.

It is believed that in the closing stages of the battle, Henry, fighting hand to hand, was in great danger. A group of Welsh knights, led by **David Gam,** intervened and saved his life. During this encounter Gam, Owain's most hated foe, was fatally wounded and was knighted as he lay dying on the field of Agincourt, by a grateful Henry. Thus fulfilling Owain's prophesy that Gam would die on a foreign field.

In 1415, **Lord Grey of Ruthin** was a member of the

Council which governed England during the absence of Henry V in France. He later fought in France in 1420 and 1421. Lord Grey died on September 30th, 1440 in Ruthin at the age of 78.

After the **Arglwyddes** was carried off to London, little was heard of her and it is believed that she died in captivity.

Catherine, together with her three daughters, accompanied the Arglwyddes into captivity. In the autumn of 1413, Catherine and two of her daughters died and were buried in St Swithin's church. The fate of the other is unknown.

When young **John Scudamore**, Owain's grandson, grew to manhood, he became a stalwart supporter of the Lancastrian cause in the War of the Roses. He fought at Mortimer's Cross and, although he escaped, his son Henry was beheaded after the battle. Edward IV refused to grant him a general pardon and he was deprived of his estates.

Sir John Oldcastle, despite his former friendship with Hal, became the instigator of a widespread Lollard conspiracy to establish a form of commonwealth. On December 14th, 1417, he was hanged in St Giles-in-the-Fields and burnt, together with the gallows on which he hung. He died a martyr. Shakespeare is said to have based the character Falstaff on Sir John Oldcastle, whose name in earlier versions of the play was Oldcastle.

Poor **Charles VI** of France continued to suffer periodic attacks of madness interspersed with short spells of sanity until his death in 1422. In 1418 his son, the Dauphin, proclaimed himself Regent of France, but was thwarted when Charles' wife, Isabella, who had gamely survived living with Charles, persuaded her husband to give his daughter Catherine in marriage to Henry V. This made Henry Regent of France and heir to the French throne. This all unravelled when Henry died and the Dauphin was eventually crowned King.

The trauma experienced by Charles when, as a young King, he was badly burnt while dancing at a ball in the palace, was considered to be the cause of his madness.

Adam of Usk received the King's pardon in 1411 and resumed his profession as an ecclesiastic lawyer. He died at Usk in 1430 and is buried in the parish church of St Mary.

Henry V died on August 31st, 1422, having contracted dysentery at the siege of Meaux.

Rhisiart and **Gruffydd** died in captivity, Rhisiart in the Bishop's prison in Worcester and Gruffydd in the Tower of London.

Dr Griffith Young made his peace with Pope Martin V and gained preferment in the church.

Maredudd was the only one of Owain's sons to survive their father. He and **Madoc** entered the King's service and unpretentiously disappeared from history.

Owain Glyn Dŵr was an eminent scholar who, in the pursuit of learning and scholarship, looked beyond the boundaries of Wales. A skilful and fierce warrior, he devoted his life attempting to establish a modern European nation. A nation which was firmly based on four foundation stones: parliament, an independent judiciary and church, freedom of speech and the autonomy of universities.

Many heirs to the English throne have been spuriously invested with the title Prince of Wales. The people of Wales acknowledge but one man who can claim the title The Last Prince of Wales and his name is Owain Glyn Dŵr.

Acknowledgements

First I must thank my editor Eifion Jenkins for his informed critique and constructive suggestions.

In writing a novel of this sort, I have had recourse to the works of many experts and I take this opportunity to record my indebtedness.

My long-standing gratitude I give to my wife, Jean, for her support and encouragement over the years.

Further Reading

Davies, R R	*Owain Glyn Dŵr* (2010)
Geoffrey of Monmouth	*The History of the Kings of Britain* (1136)
Guest, Lady Charlotte	*The Mabinogion* (*c.*1838–49)
Keegan, John	*The Face of Battle* (1976)
Lloyd, J E	*Owain Glyndŵr* (1966)
Malory, Thomas (ed.)	*The Chronicles of King Arthur* (1977)
Muntz, Hope	*The Golden Warrior* (1949)
Powys, John Cowper	*Owen Glendower* (1941)
Shakespeare, William	*King Henry IV Part One* (1597)
Starkey, David	*Crown and Country* (2010)
Voth, Grant L	*The History of World Literature* (2007)
Waugh, W T	*The English Historical Review* 20 (1905)
Williams, Glanmor	*Owen Glendower* (1966)
Williams, Gwyn A	*When was Wales?* (1985)